The Haunting of Church Cottage

Elisa Wilkinson

Published by New Generation Publishing in 2022

Front cover design by XXXXXX

First Edition

ISBN
Paperback: 978-1-80369-654-6
eBook: 978-1-80369-655-3

www.newgeneration-publishing.com

New Generation Publishing

I dedicate this book to my husband Eric and our daughter Lesley Anne.

All of the characters named in this book are fictional.

It is not what we can see
It is what we can't see
Where the truth lies

Elisa J Wilkinson

Contents

Chapter 1

THE BETRAYAL OF TRUST

The flickering light from the solid pillar candles arranged in various hollows of the dark chamber, sent eerie shadows dancing around the elaborate crypt that was to be sealed, where the corpse of the Duchess Henrietta Bartholomew would be hidden forever.

"How could you do this to me?" the Duke whispered, as leant over the beautiful woman he had married several years ago.

"I loved you, and you repaid my love by taking Thomas Outobridge, the Count of Balsbay, whom I believed to be my friend, into your bed. How could you." He seethed in bitter rage, and ground his teeth as he fought to control the embittered anger that rose in his throat.

"You deserved to die the pair of you," he snarled, revelling in the way that he'd fought and won a duel of honour with the count. Afterwards, with the help of his two loyal stewards he had dismembered the body and left the remains to be savaged by the wolves, and to rot somewhere out on the lonely North Yorkshire moors.

At the same time he'd had ordered his personal physician, whom he could trust, to systematically drug his wife with small doses of laudanum until she was completely comatose and pronounced dead. Nevertheless, even in his rage Gerard felt a solitary tear trickle down his cheek and felt the coldness of the marble slab beneath his clenched fists as he leant against the side of the sarcophagus, in torment at the knowledge of her betrayal.

As he gazed down at her remains where she lay in her white satin gown, and wearing her favourite diamond and pearl jewels that had been his gift to her on their wedding day, he felt another surge of anger charge though him and turned away unable to look at her face. He knew that any one of her three ladies in waiting could have alerted him to what was occurring behind his back, while he had been away fighting and discussing plans and strategies for the government to overthrow other foreign countries. He had had the three women poisoned, and their corpses were now chained to seats on the three separate gothic style thrones in an alcove situated in the walls of the crypt facing the marble sarcophagus containing his treacherous wife's remains.

Standing in the centre of the wall facing the door of the domed crypt, stood a gigantic statue that was carved in a likeness of himself as a Knights Templar warrior. This was so big and heavy that he knew it could never be removed and placed amongst his ancestors where he felt that it now belonged.

The massive eight feet high block of marble had been built into the wall of the crypt and carved in his likeness by a group of stonemasons, but not without a series of mishaps to the poor unfortunate masons. The walls of the chamber had then been built in a manner such that they corresponded and blended into the statue and sealed, as had the three throne like seats where the corpses of the ladies in waiting were situated.

The Duke had planned that when the time came, he and the duchess would be buried alongside one another After the disastrous discovery of his wife's infidelity he had decided that he did not wish to be buried alongside of her in their elaborately carved tomb that he had designed for them both. Instead, he'd had his own sarcophagus removed and taken to the crypt of his forefathers where he would be entombed.

After taking one last look at his wife, he ordered the coffin to be sealed and the marble lid of the sarcophagus bearing her image was slid into place above. He gave instructions to the builders to remove his own sarcophagus and rebuild it in the family vault.

The following week, after the work had been completed, Gerard locked the door of the crypt and ordered the men to seal the entrance to the tomb with stone block walling.

While the work was being carried out, no one heard the faint cries emanating from the sealed coffin inside the sarcophagus. Only Gerard understood how long it would take for the final dose of laudanum to wear off and for a person to suffocate in an enclosed space.

He left the private chapel after prayers portraying a man with a heavy heart, but hiding a smug smile of satisfaction on his face.

Chapter 2

MARY

"Yes, before you ask again, I do love you" the man whispered huskily into the thirteen year old girl's ear as he nuzzled her neck and ran his hand over her swollen belly until reaching her pubic part and began working his fingers inside her. He massaged until she was unable to withstand the excitement he was arousing in her young tender body any longer and spread her legs wide begging for him to enter her.

Mary could feel the cool moss press beneath her naked body as he rested his naked form on top of hers, then began pumping with slow rhythmical movements until he couldn't control himself any longer and began thrusting harder as she eagerly wrapped her legs around his waist. In her excitement she grabbed his heaving buttocks in an attempt to push him even further inside, until at last panting and gasping, they cried out with pleasure as they orgasmed together.

"Oh God," he whispered, between heaving breaths, "that was so good."

"I wish it could last forever," she replied, "but it could if we were married….."

He broke her off in mid-sentence.

"I will as soon as I have got enough money to support us both and the child," he said, gently caressing her cheek. Then getting to his feet he began pulling on his clothes.

Mary remained laying where she was.

"Can we do it again?" she begged in a childish pleading voice. "Please, just once again before you leave"

He turned and looked dispassionately down at her as she lay with her legs spread wide in a provocative, inviting demeanour, and despite her swollen belly, he couldn't turn his gaze away. Her youthful eagerness to please him was exciting.

I can try," he said, bending low and whispered in her ear. "Turn over and kneel."

Mary did as he asked. She enjoyed it and was thrilled when he came up with different ways of making love. She never saw the blow coming from behind as the log hit her squarely on the back of the head and caved in her skull.

"Sorry love, but there's plenty more willing girls where you came from." The man took hold of her legs and dragged her further into the underbrush to hide her body, then as a second thought he decided to fuck her one more time.

"Just for good luck," he muttered with a sadistic grin on his face.

He unfastened his pants and slid them off again, then picking up her pinny he covered her blood-soaked head and copulated with the still warm corpse.

"Now that's what I call getting rid of the evidence," he said, laughing out loud as he fastene up his pants. He gave a quick glance about the secluded area to ensure no was approaching then pulled her lifeless body deeper into the woods and covered it with loose bracken.

"I can sell these clothes, " he muttered, picking up Mary's belongings, "She won't be needing them anymore."

Chapter 3

TOM FRANKLIN

The noisy drumming of the rain hammering against the window pane of the cottage awoke eleven year old Tony Franklin, who hid beneath the covers of his bed trembling with fear. Brilliant flashes of lightning lit up the tiny bedroom which were then followed by the constant crashing of thunder that shook the cottage to its eves that he shared with his two younger brothers.

As he lay quivering beneath the ragged covers of his bed he thought of his father who would call him a coward and slap him around the head if he dared to show any sign of fear, saying that it was only a thunderstorm and an act of God.

But as his father was working away Tom ran to his mother's bedroom for comfort as had done since he was a frightened six year old. He knew that she wouldn't turn him away, she was always ready for him when his dad was absent. He was not surprised to find her bedroom door was already open to admit him, and she had lifted the bed covers as a sign of welcome to her trembling child.

As they lay there in her bed, Tom snuggled up to his mother's naked body and felt his own body relax when she placed a comforting arm around his shoulders. Then as she held him close he rested his head on her soft warm breast and within seconds his natural instinct told him what to do.

He first kissed his mother's neck as he had seen the man do to the girls in the woods, then his lips and slowly moved down her naked body until his head was between her legs. She groaned with gratification at the pleasure of what her son was giving her, knowing that her husband would never carry out such a deed saying that it was abnormal for humans to behave that way, and that it was only suitable for animals.

As his tongue probed deep inside her vagina Tom felt his mother's body arch as she climaxed, then felt her hand move down to his erect penis. Within seconds it was solid, throbbing and ready for use: this was the invitation he had waited for and within minutes he was on top of his mother, who gave a low moan of pleasure, as she guided her son inside her.

In the past, when Tom was much younger, he had kept out of sight as he followed a man into the nearby woods, who he recognised as the person who held the high position of Mayor in the local village. On each occasion, the man would check that no one was watching when he met a number of young girls and took them to the central clearing of the woods where no one ever dare venture.

From where Tom was hiding, he had the advantage of watching them strip one another of their clothing. Then they would lie down together on the soft green grass and fondle one another until the man's penis had grown to an incredible size.

Tom had watched in fascination when the man had spread the girl's legs wide open and rolled on top of her. Within minutes, they were both making strange sounds and struggling movements until the man fell, away gasping and kissing the girl fervently. In his innocence, Tom had at first thought the man was suffocating the girl and was about to run and call for help. He was shocked when he saw the girl smile and hug the man, who gave her a long lingering kiss. They then dressed and kissed once more before leaving the clearing and woodland and travelled in separate directions.

Tom did however begin to wonder why the little thing hanging down between his legs didn't grow like the man's when he lay on the girls, but as time passed by, with a little help from his mother, he began to understand.

In the following months Tom would watch as the man took many different young girls into the woods and do the same thing to each one of them. But as time went by he noticed that when each of the girl's bellies began to swell he would hear them tell the man that they were pregnant and he would have to marry them in order to give their child a name.

They had spoken their final words, for the man had a different course of action planned. He was already married and had no intention of marrying some ignorant labourer's daughter, not when he held the strong position of mayor.

He had the choice of most of the women in the village, he said to himself with a smug aura of self-satisfaction. If they became pregnant due to their promiscuous behaviour, they could blame their husbands for being the father of his unwanted offspring.

However, the day came when Tom recoiled in shock when he witnessed the first murder. The appalling event occurred after the man had cajoled the girl into a kneeling position for their sexual encounter, but as she had positioned herself the man had reached down to pick up a weapon that he had hidden nearby and beat her about the head until she died. He then threw her apron over her bloody head and as she lay on her swollen belly he had sex with her inert corpse.

Tom was almost sick as watched from his hiding place, when the man dragged the girl's lifeless body into the trees and buried her in the deepest part of the woods.

However, as Tom grew older, he would watch whatever the man did to the girls and admire the way he got rid of them without being discovered.

Over the years, Tom began imitating the man by encouraging some of the girls from the nearby cottages to go into the woods with him to play games. Then once inside their knickers, he found himself having fun until they told him he was going to be a father, and that was when he decided to copy what the man did.

He killed the girls, had sex with their corpse's then buried their bodies deep inside the wood.

Chapter 4

JANUARY 2020 THE FARM

Tim Bowman, who had hazel eyes, brown wavy hair, five foot eleven inch tall was still a good looking forty year old man who exercised regularly to stay fit. He cursed out loud as he gripped the steering wheel of his car with his big hands, as he fought to bring his vehicle, a BMW four wheel drive, under control. When he felt it slide and spin in the mud soaked deep potholed track towards the farm.

Despite the rough terrain, Tim kept a firm grip on the steering wheel until he finally negotiated his car, now caked in sludge, around the last bend to where he saw the farm house coming into view through the streaming rain and the owner of the four derelict abandoned farm cottages standing awaiting his arrival. He pulled up in the slush cluttered yard space outside.

"I only hope that the road to the cottages isn't as bad as this," Tim's friend, James Barton, grumbled. "Otherwise it will go against the asking price."

Throughout the journey James, who was a structural engineer surveyor, who owned his own company, had kept a tight hold on the hand straps as they'd bumped and bounced along the twisting terrain. He had griped non-stop throughout the entire journey, but Tim hadn't responded to James's constant moaning. However he cursed and felt a surge of revulsion sweep through him when he saw the state of the old, dilapidated buildings that had collapsed into ruin over years of neglect, along with rusted, obsolete farming equipment strewn about the yard.

"I can't believe anybody wanting to live like this there's cow and pig shit everywhere. It looks as if the place has never been cleaned up, and it stinks."

"I agree with you there," James grimaced, as the putrid stink began seeping into the car. "We'd better get moving, the rain's getting heavier and the shit's getting deeper. Come on, from the looks of the house I would say that it's almost in about as bad a state as these out buildings, he complained leaning over to the back seat and pulling their jackets over to the front of the car.

"I only hope that the cottages aren't in the same condition as this." He indicated towards the barn and out buildings, taking note of the sagging farm house roof with its missing slates, and the rotten wooden door and window frames.

Tim felt his heart sink at the thought.

"Come on," James handed Tim one of the hooded jackets, "let's get it over with. By the look of everything around here I can guess we won't be here for long. We're going to need our rubbers for wading through the shit out there."

Tim lifted the wellington boots from behind the seat and handed a pair to James.

"Your' right, we're certainly going to need these," he grumbled, taking off his shoes and pulling on the rubbers.

Chapter 5

JAKE WRIGHT THE FARMER

"We'd better get our coats on and rubbers on before we go out there, otherwise we're going to get soaked and our feet mucked up before we start," Tim added with a grimace. To be honest they were both reluctant to get out of the car.

"I can't believe what I'm seeing," he murmured, shaking his head in dismay.

"I hope to high heaven that the cottages aren't in as bad a state as this place."

"It was your idea to come, you wanted the cottages," James snapped. "So stop moaning and let's get on with it. As far as I'm concerned the sooner the deal's done and we're away from here, the better."

"You're right," Tim agreed, as they donned their jackets and rubbers before getting out of the car and stepping into the filthy mire covering the yard. They made their way along the slimy path to the house where the farmer had suddenly disappeared inside and closed the door.

"What the hell's wrong with him?"

"I've no idea," James remarked, as he knocked loudly on the door.

"All right, you don't have to break the bloody door down," they heard a raspy voice shout from inside. "I'm coming."

They heard the key turn in the lock and the door was slowly opened by the scruffy, surly old farmer, Jacob Wright, who, before they could utter a word, told them that he preferred to be called Jake, not Mr Wright, and they could call him Jake.

"He's an odd bugger," Tim whispered. "Why the devil did he run inside and shut the door when he saw us arrive?"

"Search me," James whispered back, "maybe he's afraid of strangers."

"I'm not deaf, I can hear what your'e saying, come on bring yersens in, thas letting all heat art." Jake remarked gruffly.

He opened the door just wide enough for them to enter the house then quickly slammed it shut and directed them into the stone flagged kitchen. Despite having a fire blazing in the old black cooking range the house felt as cold and damp inside as it was out.

"Well, are you going to tell me who you are, or haven't you got names?" Jake asked gruffly. James threw Tim a cautionary glance before they introduced themselves.

"Right, now I know who I'm talking to, an a know what thas come about, thad better come over here and sit down."

Tim didn't say anything as he and James followed Jake across the kitchen and sat them at a stained grubby wooden table. Then, without another word, he shuffled his bent, arthritic body into another room, mumbling that he was going to collect the documents.

This gave James and Tim the opportunity to take in their surroundings and thet noticed that the house appeared not to have been up-dated since the early 1900s.

Beside the old black range was a brick built structure that held a deep slate basin with a small fire grate beneath. James presumed that this was to heat the water that was for either taking a bath or doing the washing. He felt both were highly unlikely in the circumstances. Alongside this was a chipped, discoloured, yellow sink full of dirty unwashed pots and pans with a cast iron hand pump for pumping fresh water into the sink.

In front of the fire was an old rocking chair and foot rest, and beside the chair was a small grubby ring-stained table containing a pipe, matches, an over-filled ash tray, and a bottle of whiskey. They presumed Jake didn't bother using a glass as there wasn't one in sight. And an old Collie dog lay sleeping on hessian sacks thrown down in front of the hearth.

The kitchen was large with a low sagging wooden beamed ceiling, a bare stone flagged floor, and dirty grey whitewashed walls that had never been cleaned since the day they were painted. Hanging from extending long rusty pieces of metal that had been driven into the walls, were a number of outdated oil lamps, and others were scattered about the kitchen. These were the only source of light in the entire house.

The only furniture in the kitchen was the rickety old table and four chairs that were falling apart, which was where they were now seated. Propped against the wall of the kitchen was a high mahogany dresser with shelves at the top that were littered with papers, and the lower area that had at onetime working doors. These were now broken and hanging from their hinges, and crammed with old newspapers.

A pile of logs was heaped at the side of the fireplace along with a large number of newspapers that they assumed were for lighting the fire There were no mats or rugs on the flagged floor only torn hessian sacks that had been thrown down in places, and some were piled at the back of the door to keep out the draught.

At the corner of the far side of the kitchen was an unmade cast iron framed bed with grubby bedcovers that had been pushed up against the wall. The whole area stank of stale food, tobacco smoke, damp, and it was dismal and unwelcoming.

"I didn't realise that people still lived like this, it's bloody filthy in here," James said with a shudder, keeping his voice low.

"How old do you think he is?"

"Neither did I, to your first question, and I guess from the look of him he must be in his late seventies," Tim replied.

Before he could say anymore, Jake entered the kitchen with a carboard box filled with old papers that he thudded down onto the table sending up clouds of dust and he pulled out a number of tattered old documents.

"I've kept it all together," he said grinning through a mouth half full of blackened teeth that showed through the whiskers on his unshaven face. The whiskers partially hid his thin-lipped cruel mouth, and from the look in his hard glinting eyes it was obvious that he was a greedy, selfish man who didn't give a damn about what anybody thought of him, nor did he allow much to get past him.

Chapter 6

NEGOTIATION

"I can tell thee now that I want £200,000 for each cottage. That's eight hundred thousand for the lot and then there's the land that goes with them I want more for that.

James didn't say anything and threw Tim a look warning him to keep his mouth shut, it had been agreed before they left home that James would do all of the negotiating.

Old Jake waited impatiently as James thoroughly studied the documents for a good hour before asking to view the property. In an instant Jake quickly agreed to take them there.

"We can all go in your car," he said, rubbing his grime covered hands together.

"it will save me a bit on fuel, it's only three miles from here."

"We would prefer it if you drove ahead to show us the way to the cottages," Tim caustically replied. "Then we can take a good look around them before making our decision. If they are, as you say, three miles away from here then we will be wasting fuel returning to the farm. The return journey would add six miles on the clock, then there will be another eight to get back to the motorway. That would make it fourteen miles."

Tim didn't mention that he baulked at the idea of the dirty old man riding in his vehicle and mucking up the seats.

Jake was about to say something but stopped himself and threw Tim a scathing glower, he didn't want to miss out on a deal to make a huge sum of money and rid himself of the cottages that nobody wanted to live in let alone buy. He told them to wait while he trundled off grumbling to himself to get his motor out of the barn.

But when he drove around the corner of the barn sat on an open topped rusty antiquated tractor, they were struck dumb with disbelief.

"My God, I can't believe what I'm seeing,"

"You'd better," Tim retorted, giving a wry grin, then grimaced when Jake drove too close for comfort alongside them.

"Red diesel's cheaper" he shouted over the sound of the noisy engine, then set off down the road.

"I already despise the man," Tim ranted, as he and James knocked the filth from their boots and got into the car. He then started the engine and began following the rusty old contraption along the pot-holed road.

"Shit!" Tim cursed, "I can't see a fucking thing" he yelled as the filth from the farm track was thrown up onto his windscreen from the wide tyres of Jakes tractor.

"It's going to take an hour to get there with the speed he's doing," Tim grumbled, peering through the mud splattered windscreen.

"Don't be too sure of that, I'm certain the old devil is messing us about" James smiled reassuringly. "Anyway look at the sky."

Tim glanced up at the dark, thundery clouds overhead and nodded, then burst into a fit of laughter.

"You could be right, if the storm breaks then the silly old bugger will get soaking wet on that contraption. Maybe then he will start moving a bit faster."

The words had no sooner passed Tim's lips when the heavens opened again and the rain poured down. Within minutes, Old Jake was soaked to the skin. He put his foot down hard on the accelerator and began moving at a reasonable speed until they arrived at their destination.

Chapter 7

THE VEIWING

"Oh my God," Tim groaned, his face fell when seeing the dilapidated state of the four two storey buildings.

The four adjoining roofs were like a wavering ski-run, with old remnants of tarpaulin covering gaps where the roofing slates were missing. The wooden guttering had long since rotted away along with the frames surrounding the broken windows and doors.

"At least it is a decent road and we're not walking through sludge and muck like we were at the farm." James chuckled, trying to lighten the situation. "But I must admit the buildings are in a bloody mess."

"If he expects £200,000 for each one of those then he is off his sodding head," Tim growled in exasperation, as he stared in dismay at the dilapidated buildings.

"The whole journey has been a complete waste of time."

"Don't be too sure of that, just leave the talking to me." James gave him a reassuring smile. "I've dealt with worse people than him in my walk of life."

They sat inside Tim's car and watched as Jake hauled his rheumatoid body from his tractor and hobbled over to their vehicle,.

"We'd better get inside," Jake shouted to Tim as be banged on the car window.

"it's too wet out here to talk business,"

He turned and hurried, to the first cottage through the lopsided gate hanging from its broken hinges, and down the path that was overgrown with waist high unkempt brambles. He then fumbled with the key and opened the creaking door calling for Tim and James to get inside out of the rain.

"Good grief," was all they could say when the stench of damp and decay hit them, Tim wheeled round on Jake catching him by surprise when he asked.

"Have you been killing animals and storing their carcasses in here?" he snapped covering his nose and mouth with his handkerchief to stop the nauseating stench from infiltrating his nostrils. "It stinks like a fucking slaughter house, and It's almost as wet inside as it is out."

Jake admitted that on the odd occasion he had slaughtered a few animals and stored their carcasses in the cottages. Then without a qualm he said, "Don't worry about the water, the place will dry out when it gets a bit warmer."

Tim threw James a look of disbelief. The cottage stank, it was filthy and soaking wet, and buckets that were overflowing with water from the last downpour were scattered about the floor.

"Shit" Tim cursed then ducked out of the way when he felt water that was leaking from the floor above drip onto his head and down the back his neck.

With one quick glance they could see that the walls were just bare stone and that the whitewash that had been splashed sparsely over in them in the past was now flaking off. Obsolete gas fittings still protruded from the walls, and the panes of glass in the windows were cracked and broken. They had been boarded up in a crude attempt to stop any more of the harsh weather from entering the building. Nevertheless the rain was still pouring in, and the floor was almost two inches deep in water.

Worse was yet to come.' when they went upstairs to inspect bedrooms they were met with a torrent of water cascading down the staircase from the rain pouring in from where the roof slates were missing, "I don't believe it," Tim whispered when Jake was out of earshot.

"The whole lot should have been condemned years ago."

"Shush," James uttered in a low tone, "he's coming back. Can we inspect the cellar now?" He sked in a false, yet cheerful voice he was apprehensive at what he would find down there.

"Aye" Jake replied, "but Ide better warn thee that it's a bit wet down there He turned and led them down the staircase through the room and opened the cellar door.

James took the flashlight and shone it about the cellar.

"Bloody hell," he exclaimed when he saw it was about three feet deep in water and an accumulation of items were floating above the surface.

"I'm not going down there." James turned and made his way back up the steps and into the kitchen.

"Are all the cottages in the same condition?" he asked Jake.

"Aye" Jake replied smugly, "and they'll make a grand retreat for somebody won't they?"

"I can tell you now Jake, even if you put them up for auction you wouldn't get anything like your asking price. The lot of them require complete renovation better still they should be demolished."

"What do you mean demolished? I'm not going to let anybody pull them down"

Jake snapped angrily turning to face James.

"Jake!" James snapped into the old man's face that was now contorted with anger. "These cottages are unsuitable for habitation. You have to get planning permission if a property is to be renovated, the council planning department lay down strict laws that each building must reach certain standards to ensure that the property is habitable. I'm certain that if they saw the condition that these are in, then they would condemn the whole lot and they would have to be demolished."

Jake stared open mouthed at him in stunned silence.

"Now," James spoke in an authoritative tone.

"I would like to see the rest of the cottages if you don't mind, then I will give some thought as to what can be done with them, or better still what the land is worth when they are demolished. Then, and only then I will be able to put forward a reasonable offer."

Jake was silent as he took them to inspect each cottage and found that they were in as bad a condition as the first one they had viewed. James stood shaking his head after they had inspected the last three cottages.

"Jake I'm going to be straight with you for a start the stone in some areas has eroded and needs replacing. The roof of every cottage needs to be stripped and replaced with new matching roof slates and fitted with a good quality insulation felt that will hold in the heat. Each cottage requires new windows and doors. All of the floors have rotted away, along with the wood joists both upstairs and down. They need replacing along with the staircases. The stone flagged kitchen floors will have to be taken up and the complete area concreted and new wooden floors fitted. Also, all four cottages need re-pointing otherwise dry rot and damp will cause the cottages to deteriorate, and they will drop into the same condition as they are now.

Central heating, and electricity will be required; the ceilings and walls need to be plastered, new piping for the water supply will be compulsory for each household and there will have to be a bathroom in each cottage plus an extra indoor toilet downstairs. Also each property would require its own septic tank for the sewage waste. Plus the cellars of each cottage need the water pumping out and the walls and floors made water resistant. After close inspection I will offer you £150,000 for all four buildings and the land."

Jake began to splutter and cursed at James's offer telling him that it was a stupid price.

"I can get £200,000 when they're done up," he grumbled.

"Maybe so," James replied, "but you will have to pay that for the renovation because look at the mess they're in now."

For almost an hour the argument continued until James finally managed to reach an agreement. Jake would settle for £200,000 for all four cottages and the two acres of land they were set in, plus the small area of forest.

To ensure that Jake wouldn't go back on his word, Tim had already brought along the legal documents that he'd had drawn up by his solicitor. Then once Jake had studied the paper work he begrudgingly signed the agreement. Tim added his signature and James, acting as a witness, then attached his. As soon as they had all signed the declaration asserting Tim was now the legal owner of the four properties and land, Tim handed Jake a cheque as a deposit until the full arrangements had been drawn up by both sets of lawyers. Jake would then receive the full amount owing.

Once the deal was completed, they all got into their respective vehicles and drove away, Jake on his tractor and Tim and James in the car.

They didn't see or hear the sigh of relief that Jake gave when they were out of sight.

However, the sudden release of stress knowing that he had actually got rid of the four accursed, phantom plagued cottages, caused Jake to experience a sudden excruciating pain in his chest.

Within minutes he had doubled over in pain and had fallen from his tractor. He was crushed beneath its rear wheels as it slowly trundled away, driverless, down the steep hill.

The curse had struck again.

Chapter 8

THE WEIRD SIGHTING

"I could do with a drink after that," James said giving a sigh of relief once they were seated comfortably in the car and driving away from the repugnant old man. "Jake is one selfish, greedy old sod"

"I agree with you entirely," Tim replied. He opened the car window to take a few gasps of fresh air and to release the putrid stink of the farm out of the car, then quickly rewound the window when the full force of hail and rain hit him smack in the face.

"Shit," he cursed, wiping the dripping water away from his face with his coat sleeve, "I did notice a pub about a mile back down the road from the farm. And" he added, changing the subject, "Although Jake was asking more for what the property was worth, did you notice the look of surprise and relief on his face when we said that we would have it? To be honest, I believe that he was thankful to be getting rid of it and furthermore I think he was afraid of something."

"Now you mention it I agree, and did you notice how hesitant he was about me going down into the basement?" James commented rubbing his face thoughtfully.

"Maybe it was because of all of the water down there but from what little I saw of it, I noticed that it was deep. I can't understand though, why my light stopped working, the battery was fully charged and I'd only used it to check out the roof so the battery………"

"Shush," Tim whispered breaking into what James was about to say, and nudged his arm. "Look over there."

Tim brought the car to an abrupt halt when he saw a man with a group of young girls, wearing no outdoor clothing to protect them from the pouring rain, walking along the road about sixty yards away from where they were parked, they then disappeared into the nearby wood.

"That's weird," James muttered then became silent as he peered through the rain-lashed window to see where the strange group had gone.

"What do you think?" Tim asked, "It looks a bit odd doesn't it, do you think we should go in after them?"

"No! we will give them a few minutes, then if they don't come back this way, we'll go in and search for them." Tim agreed as he rubbed at the condensation that had settled on the windscreen when he'd switched off the engine. They sat for a few moments longer waiting for the weird group to reappear, but when they didn't, James decided they should go and search for them.

But before James could make a move to leave the car Tim grabbed hold of his arm. "Hang on a minute," he said doubtfully, "I've just realised something."

"What?"

"None of the clothing looked wet on any of them nor did their hair it was snuff dry."

"You don't think! Oh no, come on, let's get moving there's something odd going on here." The urgency in James voice sent Tim's nerves spinning when he understood what they had just witnessed. The peculiar cluster of children and the man leading them appeared to be taking a short cut through the woodland, and were heading directly towards the cottages.

Without giving a second glance towards the wood, Tim drove away as fast as he dared over the bumpy roads until he felt they were at a safe distance away from the strange sighting. He drove in silence until he abruptly pulled the car to a halt to ask James if he had noticed Jake's reaction when they went up the staircase in one of the cottages.

To his surprise, James admitted that he had noticed Jake's odd behaviour through-out the complete viewing. Also, that he himself had felt a bit on edge when sensing someone was following them about the cottages.

"Did you?" James began then stopped. "No, what I was about to say was. No! it must have been my imagination." James fell quiet.

"Did I what?" Tim asked, perplexed by his friend's hesitancy.

"I could have sworn that someone small was touching my hand in that last cottage, you know the one that was larger than the others? Did you feel anything odd about the place?" he asked Tim doubtfully.

"I'll be honest with you, yes I did, I thought I noticed someone watching us from out in the woods, but I put it down to the rain creating an illusion as it ran down the cracked window pane."

Chapter 9

ROSE OLDSWORTHY and HARRY DUCKWORTH

"I think we should call in at that pub we passed on our way here and maybe get a bite to eat I'm starving, and my feet are numb after standing for so long in the bloody cold water." James said with a grimace.

"I did notice a sign outside that said hot food served all day."

"You're right," Tim nodded as he headed back along the road they had driven earlier, "Look" James indicated and gave a sigh of relief when he saw the White Owl pub coming into view.

"Thank goodness for that, he murmured, as he noticed the sign for food was still outside as he pulled into the car park.

"We'd better get out of these stinking boots and put our shoes on. We can't go inside smelling like a pair of mucky old farmers can we?"

Tim gave him a wry look that referred to Old Jake.

They got out of the car and pulled off the boots that had been rinsed clean when they entered the water-logged cottages. Then changed into their shoes and placed the rubbers into the rear of the car.

"Bloody hell I don't believe it," James suddenly cursed when a flurry of snow-flakes began falling about their heads. "Come on let's get inside before it gets worse."

They hurried into the welcoming warmth of the pub, where they were greeted by the cheerful rosy-cheeked plump landlady. She introduced herself as Rose Oldsworthy, while at the same time eyeing and admiring both men's rugged good looks and tall strapping bodies.

"Come in gentlemen come in" she said "you look frozen, what can I get you?"

"For a start you can get us both a double scotch and a large pot of hot coffee. We need something to warm us through, and is there somewhere we can clean ourselves up a bit before we eat?" Tim asked suddenly feeling queasy as his stomach began rumbling.

Rose pointed towards the Gents Toilets.

"Thanks," he muttered, then dashed into the gents, where he opened the stall door just in time to bend over the toilet before being excruciatingly sick.

"Your friend's not very sociable is he?" Rose said loudly after Tim's rapid exit.

"He's exhausted, and we're both frozen it's been a hard day so far" James replied, glancing round at the old timber framed pub, as he gulped down the whiskey.

"I noticed the sign outside said hot food, is it too late to order anything?" he asked glancing at his watch, and noticing that it was now three thirty.

"We've still got the steak and kidney pie and veg on if you'd like it."

"That's fine, two please and two pints as well" he said pulling of his sheepskin gloves to get the money out of his pocket.

"It's alright, you don't have to pay straight away, just order what you want, you can settle up later."

"That's kind of you. By the way how long has this place been here?" he asked as he took off his woolly hat and dashed the snow from it.

"The pub? Oh, it was built in the early eighteen hundred's, but bits have been added on throughout time, you know bringing it up to date. Part of it was rebuilt from an old house that used to stand over there where the games room is. It's mostly farmers that we get in here and hikers throughout the summer."

"I see, well thanks for that," James gave her one of his charming smiles and almost laughed when she grabbed hold of the bar to keep herself upright at the unanticipated compliment.

As James made his way over to the table near the blazing fire he saw that Tim was now seated, warming his hands. He did, however, notice an elderly man sitting on his own by the fire exit and walked over to speak to him.

"Would you care to join us?" he asked, indicating towards Tim, "I think you will be much warmer over by the fire."

"I'm James Barton and that is my friend Tim Bowman, you look lonely sitting here on our own, and it's cold over here," he added, glancing around at the semi-lit area.

"Could I get you a drink?"

"No," but thanks all the same. I'm Harry Duckworth." He spoke with a broad Yorkshire accent as he held out his hand in a friendly gesture.

"You're not from around here are you? From the way you're dressed, you're, not hikers either."

James smiled at the old man's questions as he shook hands with him.

"We've just been up to the old farm to look at the cottages that Jacob Wright is selling."

"Old Jake" Harry puffed at his pipe and sneered when saying the man's name.

"Nobody with any sense around here has anything to do with him, he's a nasty old bugger that one. After his wife died he shut himself off from the village, it was her who everybody liked not him. We all felt sorry for her, she was a nice woman, too good for the likes of him if you ask me. What the Dickens she saw in him heaven only knows because he led her a dog's life." Again, he sniffed disdainfully.

"I don't suppose you got anywhere with him?"

"As you said," James was suddenly alert and on his guard. "Mr Wright isn't a very easy person to deal with, especially when it comes to money."

Harry gave a sly, toothless grin. "So you have been looking at them their cottages have you?"

"You could say so," James replied, "in fact my, business partner and I have just purchased all four cottages."

"Mercy me," Harry gasped, clutching his hand to his chest.

"I can't believe it, Old Jake selling them cottages. Mind you nobody in the village would touch them. I bet he asked for a tidy sum?. What did he want for them?"

"Sorry, that would be telling wouldn't it? Besides what we paid for them is between old Jake, Tim and me, and nobody else."

"Well, I'll tell you something, you'd have been better off leaving them be, they should have been pulled down years ago and the land thoroughly salted to exorcise all the demons abiding there. The whole place is as haunted as hell, and the forest around it. You won't get any locals wanting to live there, and you won't get any help from anybody around here either pulling' em down or doing' em up."

Just then Rose called that the food was on the table.

"Excuse me but I've got to go, I don't want the food to go cold," James excused himself and returned to the table.

"Were you out at old Jakes site?" Rose asked with a hint of uncertainty in her tone. "If so, I'd advise you to keep your distance from there. It's a bad place and anybody in their right mind won't ever go near it. Even old Jake who owns it avoids the place."

"Oh no, just give me a few minutes," she grumbled, glancing towards a man who was waiting impatiently to be served and was banging his empty tankard up and down on the bar counter.

"I'll come over and tell you in a few minutes what happened there, and why nobody wanted the cottages."

Rose returned to the bar to serve the customer who began complaining that she was only interested in the newcomers and didn't care about the regulars.

Meanwhile, James was now seated at the fireside table with Tim, but, in no time at all everyone was staring at them with strange looks on their faces, and whispering in quiet undertones.

"I'll bet Rose is already gossiping." James, declared with a grimace.

Chapter 10

THE HISTORY OF THE COTTAGES

"Right gents," they heard Rose say when she re-appeared and flopped down onto the seat beside them. "I'm going to tell you about those cottages."

Tim and James looked at one another and gave a sigh of resignation as she began speaking.

"In the late 1700s there was a big house standing where the cottages are now, but due to the Lord and Lady Bartholomew not having any children the house stood empty after they died and nobody wanted to live there. The people who did move in quickly left the place saying it was haunted, and in time it became derelict and repairs were urgently needed to keep the Hall in a reasonable condition.

After a few years, the authorities were unable to contact anyone connected to the property, so the parish took it on and cleared the site and built a church there that was run by Vicar Hallston and his wife, Alice. They had five children, all under the age of ten. Alice did all the flower arrangements for funerals and weddings; she polished the brass, and did all the cleaning, she kept everything spick and span. It was rumoured that he never gave her and the children enough food to eat and they were practically starved by the vicar who was a mean, nasty old bugger."

"Anyway, one day something bad happened, he went mad. He took a knife and starting with Alice, he cut her throat and did the same with each of the youngsters. Then he killed his sister-in law and the two dogs. He butchered them just like Old Jake does with his sheep. Then to avoid detection he hid their bodies in the crypt and told people that Alice had taken the children to visit relatives for a month in Scotland.

As far as the villagers knew she didn't have any relatives in Scotland, Alice was a local lass."

"Hang on a minute," Tim voice was strained as he spoke. He looked at James who was sat staring at Rose with his mouth gaping wide open in disbelief.

"You are telling us that he murdered his entire family?"

"That's right, he did' em all in, every last one of 'em, even her cousin who was visiting and both dogs. Anyhow, when they hadn't been seen for some time, the villagers got suspicious and started asking questions that he couldn't answer. So one day they stormed the church and found the bodies rotting in the crypt. They were so infuriated at what he'd done they burnt the church down, stripped the vicar, flogged him, then hung him in the nearby woods."

"Bloody hell!" James exclaimed loudly.

"So what happened then?" he asked, dreading what she was going to say next.

"Well, as far as we know, nobody was willing to bury him so they left him there to rot."

For a moment the men sat staring at Rose in disbelief, unable to comprehend what she was saying, before Tim uttered, chuffing hell," in a rasping tone. While James remained speechless.

"Anyway," Rose continued, apparently unconcerned about how her words were affecting the two men.

"The church bell was taken away and thrown into the big lake over one hundred miles away from here, and everything inside the church was burnt in the fire.

In time, the church commissioners decided to turn the ruins into four cottages. They used the old church stone, put a new roof on it and cleaned the place up, but nobody wanted to live there. So Old Jake's ancestors bought them. I can tell you the church was only too pleased to get shut of them. Anyhow, over the years he couldn't get anybody to live there for any length of time, and anybody who did try didn't stay for very long."

"Why," James asked glancing nervously over at Tim, who was sat white faced and speechless staring at Rose. He wanted to know as much as he could about the property especially about the hauntings.

"Well!" Rose continued, "the locals said there was incest in one of them cottages and one of the lads, Thomas Franklin, who lived there was a killer. He was caught bashing a thirteen year old pregnant girl's head in with a lump of wood. He confessed to putting her in the family way and had killed her because he was too young to be married, and he didn't want to be tied down with a squalling brat. He then bragged that he'd done the same to others. He took the authorities deep into the woods and showed them where he had buried the bodies, just like the man had."

"When they asked who the man was he gave the Village Elders name, Dennis Heslop, who was the presiding councillor and judge over the entire community.

At first they didn't believe him, as it was a serious accusation he was making. They were about to hang him right there and then, until some of the villagers came forward to say that their teenage daughters had been seen with Heslop before going missing. But when they had reported the disappearance to the police, they were told that the girls must have left the village to find a better position in life and the police didn't bother to do anything about it."

Tim felt a surge of anger run through him, "Surely somebody took notice of what was happening?"

"None of them cared, they didn't give a damn about what happened to the poor people in the community. All the top nobs were bothered about was money and protecting their names." Rose added huffily.

"It's the same today, they say that money talks louder than words."

Tim couldn't help but agree.

"Anyway back to what I was saying, part of the woods belong to whoever owns the cottages and they are haunted as well, so everybody avoids them places. We've all seen the vicar's ghost and Tom's watching us from the wood, and some have even seen young girls going in there and not coming out."

James felt his blood grow cold and shuddered at what she was saying, realising that it had not been his imagination when he thought there had been someone watching them from the woods. For a moment he couldn't think of anything to say and glanced over at Tim who was sat staring at him with a frozen look on his face. He recalled them both seeing the man and young girls going into the woods.

Over the years," Rose rambled on, "the cottages became derelict as nobody wanted to live there because of what had happened in the past."

"Oh, excuse me a minute, I've got another customer waiting,"

Heaving herself to her feet Rose waddled over to the bar to pull a pint for the customer, leaving Tim and James stunned and worrying about what they had let themselves in for.

But when she returned, it was Rose who was the one in for a shock, when James told her that he had been speaking to Harry Duckworth shortly before she had brought the food to the table.

Her face blanched, "Harry Duckworth? Old Harry? you were talking to him.? But you couldn't have been,"

"Yes I was, James told her," as he turned and pointed to the now empty table.

"He was seated over there"

"Oh my God" she groaned, "Harry's been dead and gone for nigh over seven years now. That was his favourite table, he always sat there supping his pint, and puffing his pipe."

James looked at her in bewilderment.

"Where you say he was sitting is near the games room, and the stone they built that with came from old Harry's house."

Chapter 11

RECONSTRUCTION

The sale of the cottages went through without any complications apart from the unexpected death of Jake, the old farmer. His only surviving relative whom he hadn't seen in years tried to extract a higher payment for the surrounding land.

But when Tim's lawyers produced a copy of the document that Jake had signed. The relative found that he couldn't do anything to procure more money from Jake's estate and he settled for the sum paid.

It took six months of haggle with the council, who did their utmost to interfere and delay the renovation, because they were private individuals and not a big building concern, before they reluctantly gave the go-ahead and work was started on the refurbishment of the properties.

Tim, who was an architectural engineer, had drawn up the plans for the buildings restructure. He had redesigned the configuration of all four cottages and had extended the building at the rear and rearranged the complete framework so that it was now one compact building. His friend, James Barton, a building surveyor, had ensured that all of the footings were safe, then after the planning permissions were granted, he sent a team of workmen to carry out the full renovations of the property.

The first big problem however, was the roof; on close examination they found that most of the roofing slates were cracked and broken whereby the whole roof had to be replaced, but the old oak supporting beams were still as solid as the day they were placed there. All they needed was cleaning and a protective layer of creosote painting over them to enable them to last for another hundred years or more.

Generators for electricity were transported there, and portable arc lights were placed about the cottages to enable the work gang to see what they were doing. Also commercial pumps had been brought in to remove the knee deep water from the huge cellar. As soon as the water was extracted from the cellar, the items that were floating there had been removed and stored in one of the old out-buildings. The builders were now using these for the storage of the works equipment.

Each separate cottage had a locked door that opened onto a stone staircase consisting of seven wide stone steps. Each flight of steps was fitted with a wooden hand rail on either side that led down to the huge, dark, windowless communal cellar. This was where the laundry and preparation of slaughtered animals had been carried out.

There were four deep yellow sinks with stone draining boards on either side with hand pumps fitted over them. James presumed that the two large cast iron hand pumps for the water supply at the top area of the cellar had been used for rinsing the water away after washing any unwanted fluids from the animals' bodies after they had been slaughtered. The deep gulley running along the skirting of the cellar to the outside of the building would have been the drainage channel.

There were four large slate pots for boiling hot water with a fire grate beneath them. Three fire grates for heating a large number of different sized irons that had been abandoned by previous owners, and a number of pulleys hanging from the ceiling to dry the linen and clothes on a wet day. There were also four long metal baths that were suspended by hooks that were driven deep into the walls. All of these items were now removed and placed in safe storage along with the other relics.

There was also a solitary door leading outside the cellar to a flight of seven, ten feet wide stone steps. These steps led up to the back garden where the clothes would have been hung out to dry, weather permitting.

Along one side of the cellar were huge stone slabs, these, Tim presumed, were probably used for preparing the slaughtered animals and birds for market.

In a corner of the basement, lying on a flat stone slab, were a number of rusty old paraffin lamps, flint boxes and candles that had fused together over the years, and long perished tapers that fell to pieces as soon as Tim handled them.

Tim assumed that they must have been used to light up the cellar when the women were working there.

It took a full week to drain the cellar of the flood water that had amassed there, and to remove the old artifacts. All four stone staircases were removed and a new modern one was built alongside the wall for access into the basement.

Once this was completed the foreman could then examine the floor and walls for any structural damage. He set about sealing the whole area ensuring that it was completely water tight. However, as the men had been removing the stone staircases they had discovered a low iron studded oak door that had been hidden beneath one of the sets of stairs. This had previously gone unnoticed due to its position in the darkness, plus the algae that had accumulated there over the years that was now covering the walls. Along with this, the door had been concealed by the same grubby whitewash that had been splattered over the walls in the past, making it almost undetectable to the naked eye.

Nevertheless, Tim was excited about the unusual discovery and asked Bill, the Foreman, if he had seen what was behind the door. Bill shook his head, as he presumed that the door was either locked or swollen from the water that had swamped the cellar during the winter months as he couldn't get it open.

This left them with only one option and that was to force it open, but no matter how hard Tim and Bill pulled they couldn't move the door. Therefore, the only alternative left was for Tim to bring in a locksmith as there was no key. Plus, he didn't want to cause any further damage to the door beyond what the water had already caused.

Chapter 12

THE LOCKSMITH

It took Tim two days to locate a locksmith who was willing to come to the cottage and a further seven days waiting for him to arrive. As soon as he came Tim whisked him down into the cellar and showed him the door.

"Do you think you can open it?" he asked, impatient to see what was on the other side.

"In time sir, you must be patient," the locksmith replied, as he opened up his case that held a substantial amount of old antique keys and other paraphernalia.

Tim watched along with a group of labourers who were equally as anxious to see what was behind the door, as the man systematically tried numerous keys before indicating that he had found one that fitted. Then using a specialist oil, he sprayed inside the lock, the key, then the door hinges. He then applied a rust removing substance to soften the corrosion before he could go any further. After almost half an hour of waiting he began scraping the flaking substance away from the hinges. He next carefully manipulated the key until it finally turned in the lock and eased the door slowly open so they didn't damage it.

"Bloody hell," the locksmith gasped immediately leaping back with a look of sheer horror on his face as the door creaked slowly open, and a dark image followed by a fetid stink brushed past them.

The locksmith was beside himself with fear and on the verge of hysteria due to the unexpected terrifying experience. He threw an anxious look at Tim then over to the team of workers who were stood paralyzed with fear at what they were seeing.

"Sorry gov," he stammered, " that's it for me, I'm done. I've heard the rumours about this place and I'm out of here. I'll send you the bill" with that he hastily departed the way he had entered, leaving the key behind him in the lock.

Tim watched speechless along with the team working in the cellar as the man scarpered away. Nevertheless, the strange, uneasy looks that passed between the men and the mumbles of apprehension caused Tim to feel a sense of unease himself.

Whatever the men were feeling they didn't say anything, but there was an air of disquiet about them and Tim wasn't too happy about it. Regardless of the atmospheric change that had suddenly descended in the cellar, Tim decided to go ahead and investigate what was in the room below. But after giving some thought of to what could be waiting for him down there in the dark, Tim's bravado suddenly ebbed away and he became undecided as to what he should do.

"Sod it," he mumbled to himself, "I'm going in there."

Calling on his sense of bravado, Tim stepped forward and switched on the light of his mobile phone and shone it into the heavy impregnable gloomy area. He noticed four wide stone steps leading down into a dark empty space, but as soon as he descended the first of the steps, Tim realised from the low roof and the narrowness of the stone walls that it must have led to the crypt. This was where the vicar had hidden the remains of his slaughtered family; it would also have been part of the ruined church.

Tim hesitated for a few moments before descending the rest of the steps and found himself standing in a confined area. He felt his skin crawl at the thought of what had occurred there.

Did Vicar Halston kill his entire family in the crypt ? Or did he slaughter them in the church? and whereabouts in the crypt did he hide their bodies.?

"Oh shit," he groaned. "I should never have come down here on my own." Tim stood undecided as of what to do next.

"For goodness sake," he mumbled to himself, "pull yourself together and stop being such a bloody coward."

Taking a deep breath, Tim stepped forward and shone the thin beam of light about the crypt noticing that the roof was arched and low, creating a sense of claustrophobia in the dank, dismal chamber surrounding him. He assumed that in the past, the three four foot high stone slabs set along the length of two of the walls had been used for the placement of coffins for the deceased clergy. claustrophobic.

However, finding himself standing in oppressive darkness Tim suddenly sensed that he was not alone, as he felt something cold touch his arm. Something, or somebody, whom he couldn't see, was standing close beside him.

"Oh God!" he screamed when an unwarranted sense of anxiety and fear that he had never felt in his entire life completely flooded his terrified mind.

In a near panic Tim turned and swung the light about the crypt, but as it was just a slim beam of light he could only visualise a conflicting mixture of dancing shadows that only increased his sense of fear and unease.

Within seconds he was out of the crypt, and was speedily followed by the men who had been working there up the stairs and out of the cellar.

Chapter 13

RENOVATION

Tim managed to push aside the alarming incident in the crypt and concentrated on rebuilding the property. A ten foot extension had been added to the rear of the property along with a triple garage. A new plumbing system was fitted along with gas and electricity. New double glazed windows and doors were installed and the forty foot long room at the end of the building where the services had been held was changed into a spacious kitchen come dining area. A section of the room was partitioned off to be used as the utility room.

The four staircases in each cottage were removed and replaced by a single one that wasn't as steep, and recycled two inch thick solid oak wooden floors boards were laid in each room.

The staircase led onto a landing to each bedroom, and a telephone table and seats had been placed in the open area at the bottom of the staircase. The wall of the connecting second and first cottage had been knocked through at the rear and were now converted into a second lounge, with patio doors leading onto the lawned garden. The rooms at the front had been furnished and were to be used as separate offices for himself and Julia, and a spare room. Upstairs, the large bedroom was converted into an en-suite with a walk in wardrobe and fitted cupboards and drawers. The spacious children's bedrooms were identical to that of their parent's, both children wanted the rooms at the rear of the property overlooking the beautiful scenic view from the rear of the cottage. The other three bedrooms at the front remained empty and a bathroom for guests was at the end of the balcony.

The cellar had been divided and a partition was built! the first area was changed into a games room with a large snooker table and a bar for Tim to entertain his friends and business colleagues. The other half was fully kitted out with gymnasium equipment, and both floors had been covered by similar oak boarding to that which was upstairs and carpeted. The crypt door was kept locked, and was hidden behind a screen and forgotten about.

A large double garage had been built and attached to the side of the cottage, with a connecting door to the kitchen. Tim had added a downstairs toilet, and a new septic tank with a soakaway had been fitted underground away from the cottage. The stone built well in the centre of the garden had been sealed at the top so no-one could fall down it, and Tim had an electric pump installed to draw water for the garden.

Finally, the whole structure was sand blasted to remove the grime and dirt from the aged, blackened stone.

Within eight months all of the work had been completed.

Chapter 14

THE HAUNTINGS

Regardless of the change for the better in the weather, the labourers had been uncomfortable working at the cottage. They often complained of someone standing nearby watching them as they worked, but upon checking to see who it was, they found no one there. There was also the sound of dogs barking, and children giggling and shrieking as they raced from one room to another around the cottages and gardens. Yet as soon as the workmen neared the area where the sounds were coming from, the noises ceased, leaving them nervous and uncomfortable.

They had all heard the rumours of the cottages being haunted when they called in at the White Owl pub, and had laughed at what they were hearing. But after noticing the vague figures of two men and a group of young pregnant women standing amongst the trees nearby watching them as they worked outside, the men had become concerned when the figures they had evaporated into a mist and disappeared into the woody area as they approached them.

The landscape gardeners were also scared when they saw a number of young children's faces staring at them from inside the windows of the converted property while it was still unoccupied. Children were also seen skipping and cavorting about the gardens with two black dogs that vanished directly they were approached.

Then there was the beautiful woman wearing a full length cream coloured gown who appeared from out of nowhere. She was often seen carrying a flat wicker basket filled with flowers as she floated gracefully along the road on the outskirts of Tim's property.

But the worst sight of all was the ashen faced, emaciated woman, who would appear unexpectedly and follow the men about with outstretched arms as if appealing for help before suddenly disappearing through the wall of the house.

"To be honest," Frank had said, "he was relieved when the work was completed and he could get his men away from there."

Chapter 15

LOCAL SUPERSTITION

The first impression Julia had of the cottage was love at first sight, and the children Rupert, 20, and Annabella, 18, adored it from the first moment of seeing it. It's quaint appearance and shape gave it the look of a magic, enchanted cottage with the woodland forest behind.

A crazy-paved stone path with long, scented wisteria and clematis covered floral arches, led through a wide arched gate with lawns trees, colourful shrubs, and flowers on either side. At the rear of the cottage, set in the centre of the lawned garden, was a well-stocked fish pond, as well as an orchard set with a variety of fruit trees. There was also a huge greenhouse for Tim to grow tomatoes, and to plant seeds so that he could grow his own vegetables and flowers.

However they were unaware that at one time the huge gardens at the rear of the property had once been a cemetery. After the murders everyone in the village had believed that the church and its grounds were no longer sanctified. The bodies of their deceased relatives and ancestors had been removed, and their remains were interred in freshly dug graves. The gravestones had also been taken and rebuilt in the new churchyard.

Unbeknownst to them, at the extreme furthest point of the land that was overrun by thick bush and heavy undergrowth that had yet to be cultivated, was a stone engraved tomb dedicated to Alice and the five children who were buried there along with their aunt. In addition to this was memorial to the two faithful dogs that had tried unsuccessfully to protect Alice and the children from her brutal husband before being slain themselves.

Due to ancient superstition, the locals believed that a suicide or a murdered person's soul would not find peace and would rise up from the dead until justice was done.

Otherwise, they would haunt the area where they had met their deaths. Therefore, Alice the children and her sister could not be buried in consecrated ground.

There was, however, no mention of her insane, murderous husband to be found in the surrounding area. It was if he had never existed as no parish records could account for where he was born or where he had died.

Chapter 16

MOVING IN

The first few weeks of settling in at the cottage were hectic Rupert stayed home for just a few days before returning to the academy where he was training to become an officer, while Annabella was studying medicine at university where she was focused on become a specialist in gynaecology.

Julia owned several beauty salons consisting of hairdressing, different types of relaxation therapies, massage, nail, beauty and skin treatments and sauna. She was beginning to feel the pressure and was totally exhausted after a full day's work. But although she employed managers to run the shops, the pressure of moving house and running the businesses were beginning to take a toll on her.

The stress and tension of having customers who constantly pressurised and bombarded her with complaints and enquiries, was beginning to wear her down.

Then to crown it all, Tim, who was constantly hinting that she wasn't getting any Younger, had suggested that she should hand over the reins to someone else.

However, without Tim's constant nagging, Julia had already decided to put into action what she was planning to do. Four of the most experienced ladies who had been in her employ for a number of years had asked if they could take over the running of four of her beauty salons. Julia was pleased as this gave her the opportunity to settle down and concentrate on carrying out the legal paperwork involving Judy, Maddy and Amy, the three young beauticians she employed, who wanted to start up in business for themselves. They had asked if they could jointly purchase the business franchise of her shop at Ripon, and to take out a lease and pay Julia a monthly rent for the property.

Both she and Tim had thought this was a good idea, and would give them more time to spend together as a family.

Chapter 17

STRANGE PHENOMENA

"Oh no, it's raining again" Julia grumbled as she noticed the unexpected cloud burst of rain streaming down the window pane.

"I hope it's only a passing shower," she mumbled to herself, and carried on sorting through the paperwork on her desk.

Then something unusual occurred, Julia, who was accustomed to having pets around her had waited to get settled in before asking her friend Teressa to bring their two dogs and cats to the cottage. While she was working Julia had felt something nudge against her leg, and felt the warmth of an animal's body pressing against her thigh. Without thinking, Julia had automatically reached down to stroke the soft fur of a dog's head, then stopped when suddenly realising that the dogs were still in Harrogate.

"Oh shit," she muttered quietly and glanced down sideways where it was obvious nothing was there. For the first few moments Julia remained motionless unsure of what to do before very slowly getting to her feet. Then on shaking legs she wobbled over to the door, opened it, and hurried out into the open area, slamming the door shut behind her.

Panic stricken, Julia ran screaming into her husband's study, but ground to a sudden halt when seeing him sitting at his desk motionless, staring with a strange expression on his face at the shelving on the wall where his files were stored.

"Tim," she croaked in a voice that was constricted in terror after her fearful encounter.

"Tim, for God's, sake speak to me!" she screamed at the sight of his ashen face.

Pushing aside her own frightening experience, Julia moved cautiously towards her husband and touched his arm but there was no response.

"Oh no, what do I do?" she whispered anxiously, Julia was confused and she couldn't understand what was happening.

"Tim," "Tim," she shouted, pulling at his arm, "What is it? What's wrong?"

All of a sudden he responded and stared at Julia with a bewildered expression on his face.

"Oh God," he moaned as he slowly regained his senses, then he gave a gasp of alarm and leapt to his feet shaking from head to toe, staring fitfully about the room.

"Did you see them?" he stuttered, pointing a trembling finger towards the wall.

"They went through there, did you see them?"

"Tim what are you talking about? there's no one in here but you and me."

"No, that girl and the dog, they went straight through the wall." He spoke in a soft undertone as if not wanting to be overheard by anyone, yet even so his voice was filled with hysteria and he was shaking badly.

"Tim calm down," she commanded in a stern tone. "Tell me exactly, what did you see?"

Tim stared at her for a few moments rubbing his head in frustration before managing to control himself.

"I'm sorry love," he began "I didn't mean to upset you but they took me completely by surprise."

"Who?" Julia asked. "What are you talking about?"

Tim stared at her for a few moments before answering.

"I was working on the design for the new market when I started to feel odd, if that's the word for it. So I thought that rather than disturb you I would go and make a pot of tea for us both, but just as I was about to get up I glanced over to the wall, and I'm not kidding you I got the shock of my life when I saw a girl come straight through the wall followed by a big black dog."

"They went straight past me as if I didn't exist and disappeared through the wall over there." He stared in dread at the wall as if expecting them to reappear.

For a moment Julia believed that Tim was going to be ill as he fought to control the fear that was threatening to overtake him.

"Tim, why don't we have that cup of tea then I will tell you about what happened in my office." she said calmly moving towards him and taking his arm.

"What do you mean? What you have seen? Was it the same as m......"

Julia broke him off in mid-sentence.

"Let's get the tea, then I will explain."

"No!" he snapped, pulling his arm away from her grasp.

"What you've got to say? I want to hear now."

Julia realised that he wouldn't wait for an answer. "Alright, I will tell you, I felt something lean against my leg in my office and it felt like a dog so I stroked its head, I could actually feel its soft fur beneath my fingers, but when I looked down it wasn't there. I panicked and ran to tell you what had happened, but when I reached your office, I saw that you were in a worse state than me."

Tim stood shaking his head. "I'm sorry sweetheart I didn't mean to snap, I really mean it, I am sorry and I feel so bloody stupid."

"Don't worry about it, darling," Julia took his arm again and began guiding him through into the kitchen.

"Let's have a cuppa and try to work things out; there has to be a reasonable explanation somewhere."

Chapter 18

A CRY FOR HELP

"Have you thought of anything?" Julia asked the all-important question as they sat drinking their tea.

Tim was about to reply when they were unexpectedly interrupted by the sound of laughter and a dog barking coming from their front garden.

"Who the devil can that be in this weather?" Tim grumbled as he got up from the seat, and went over to the window and peered out through the rain-streaked glass.

"I don't believe it, there's a bloody stupid woman out there in the pouring rain playing ball with a dog on our front lawn."

"What?" Julia said angrily. "You have to be joking."

Julia strode over to the window and rapped on the glass to gain the woman's attention, but the woman ignored her and carried on chasing around the garden with the dog.

Her ill-mannered action infuriated Julia who went to the door to shout to her, but by the time she had opened the door, the woman and the dog were gone.

"Where did she go?" Tim asked, surprised by the woman's sudden disappearance.

"She was there a minute ago."

"I've no idea," Julia replied. "But she had no right to be in our garden."

"Hum," he responded with a shrug, then turned and began moving away, but stopped abruptly when Julia screamed and grabbed hold of him and pointed towards the window.

"Tim, look" her voice was almost a whimper as she spoke.

Tim turned and almost yelled himself when he came face to face with a ghastly, spectral grey faced, hollow-eyed woman who was peering in at them through the window.

"Bloody hell" he shouted and reached out to close the drapes. "It's alright Julia, she's gone, she can't hurt us."

Tim grabbed hold of his wife who was shaking and sobbing with fright in an attempt to calm her, while at the same time wishing that someone could do the same for him.

Nevertheless, as much as he tried, Tim couldn't hide the fact that he was just as shaken and afraid as his wife.

"Come on old thing let's sit down," he said, glancing warily about the room as he led Julia over to the sofa and seated her, then sat down beside her.

"Did you notice the way she was dressed?" he asked thoughtfully. "She looked like somebody from. Oh shit no!" he exclaimed loudly.

Julia watched as a look of fear and disbelief spread across his face when it suddenly dawned on him who they had just seen.

"Do you recall hearing about Alice Halston the vicar's wife?"

"Yes" Julia replied, "didn't her husband murder her and his entire family?

"Yes, he did, and Rose Oldsworthy, who keeps the White Owl Pub, told James and me that on the odd occasion, Alice Halston had been seen in the garden with her two dogs at the old church cottages. I think we have just seen Alice's ghost out there in the garden."

Julia's hands shot to her mouth as a look of realization spread across her face.

"Oh dear God, no," she cried, giving a long strangled groan.

"Please, please don't let her haunt us and the house, please." With a look of disbelief on her face Julia crumpled into the chair sobbing.

"Sweetheart, she hasn't done anything to harm us," Tim spoke in a condescending tone.

"I know that," Julia cried, "but I can't stand the thoughts of living with a ghost."

"Julia! Listen to me, just for a moment, please, listen to me," he said grabbing her flailing arms. "I know somebody who can help, just calm down and listen."

Julia stopped ranting and glared at him.

"It's all your fault," she snapped. "Surely you must have heard rumours or something before you agreed to buy the property."

"Please believe me, I didn't, now will you please be quiet for a moment, calm down and listen to what I have to say."

Tim tried to keep the tone light as he spoke, although he felt like slapping her.

"We know for certain that no one will come from the village to help, but I do know a man who can help us! David Hartley, you remember him don't you? he is the vicar at our old church, St Bartholomew's."

"Of course I remember David," she snapped. "He and his family came to tea often enough didn't they?"

"God, give me strength," Tim uttered silently, forcing himself to hold his patience, as it appeared that Julia hadn't thought for a moment that the weird phenomenon had upset m also. Nevertheless, at that moment he had to use every amount of composure to stop himself from panicking and to pacify his distraught wife.

"Right," Tim said decisively taking a defiant stance. "Maybe David can bless the cottage and help to lay the ghost to rest, what do you say?"

To his surprise Julia thought it was a good idea and agreed.

"Great, I will ring him right away, I've got his number in my office, I'll have a word with him and explain what has happened, maybe he can help us."

Tim hurried from the room to search for his notebook containing all of the contact numbers of his friends and business acquaintances.

"Tim" he heard Julia speak from the doorway, "why don't you simply use your mobile to find his number, that way it will be quicker."

"What? Oh yes you're right," he replied smiling at her. "I didn't think of that" Tim pulled the mobile from his pocket and began scrolling for David's number.

"Got it" he said triumphantly and pressed in the number.

"Shit, it's a bloody voice mail," he ranted, slamming the phone down.

"Well you should have left a message you idiot then he would have come back to you."

Chapter 19

JESSICA HOWARD

Just then the doorbell rang causing them both to jump with fright.

"Bloody hell not now," Tim cursed. "It can't be the postman at this time of day, anyway he wouldn't come to the door."

The postman would only deliver the mail on the proviso that they placed the mail box at the garden entrance. Otherwise they would have to pick up their mail from the village post office as no one was willing to go anywhere near the cottage.

Julia threw Tim a fearful glance and hesitated for a moment before going over to the Window, dragging Tim along with her. Then after ensuring he was standing close by her side she tweaked the lace curtain slightly allowing them both to see who was there through the rain spattered glass. She was surprised to see a drenched middle-aged woman dripping water everywhere in the wooden foyer at the back door.

She was wearing a see through plastic mac with a hood over her dark blue coat, and a colourful headscarf covering her hair. Her boots were covered in sludge from the long trek up the mud splattered road, and she was holding a covered basket in her hands.

"I wonder what she wants?" Julia said apprehensively, turning and looking at Tim..

"Do you think she is real?"

"Well, there is only one way to find out" he replied going into the hall towards the door with Julia following behind.

"I'm scared," she whispered softly. "You know we don't have visitors from the village."

He turned towards Julia. "It's alright sweetheart, she doesn't look like anybody we know from the village. Now stop fretting and I'll go see what she wants."

Nevertheless Tim was filled with apprehension as he turned the key to unlock the door and opened it. To his surprise he was greeted with a cheery hello from a short, plump, ruddy-complexioned, middle aged woman standing at the door with a pleasant smile on her face.

"Hello, are you Mr Bowman?" she enquired.

"That's me," Tim replied, "can I help you?"

"I'm Jessica Howard," she said. "I believe that I have found something that you may find interesting, and could also be of great importance to you."

For a minute she hesitated as she saw a dubious look cross Tim's face.

"Before you shoo me away and close the door on me, I really do think you should see these."

Jessica lifted the waterproof wrap to reveal a number of documents swathed in a plastic cover packed on top of another pile of papers and waved it in his face.

"It is regarding this cottage when it was the local church, before and after it was burnt down by the local villagers. Also some old hardly recognisable photographs of the ruins when it was being turned into cottages."

She glanced into the hallway. "Would it be all right if I came in, it's a bit wet out here and I need to keep these documents dry."

Jessica fumbled in her basket for a few moments before bringing out a handful of documents wrapped in a plastic folder from her basket.

"You need to see these," she said wafting them under his nose. Immediately Tim's curiosity was aroused.

"I think you had better come in out of the rain" he said noticing the puddle she was now standing in and opened the door wider for Jessica to enter.

"Thank you" she said, "I will leave my boots here if you don't mind they are a bit muddy from the walk. That farmer never cleans the road," she remarked huffily as she straightened her clothing.

Jessica slid off her muddy boots and stepped inside away from the blustery wind and rain, leaving Tim to struggle with the door against the force of the strong wind that had now arisen and he slammed it shut behind her.

"Let me take your mac and coat,"

Tim helped her out of her wet clothing and hung it in the hall, while at the same time noticing that she gave the impression of someone who was a little eccentric by the garments she was wearing.

Regardless of her appearance he could see that she was an extremely intelligent woman and she had good taste in clothing, although from the look of it, it appeared to have been purchased from a quality charity shop.

Julia suddenly appeared with a pair of slippers in her hand.

'Oh my goodness,' she thought, 'the woman looks like Margaret Rutherford who played the part of Madame Arcati in Blyth Spirit.'

Smiling and stifling a giggle, Julia held out the slippers and told Jessica to put them on otherwise her feet would be cold.

"Would you like a cup of tea or coffee? you look frozen."

"I don't want to put you to any trouble, but I wouldn't say no to a nice cup of tea."

Jessica took the slippers and slid them onto her feet then followed Julia into Tim's office.

"My you have made a good job of the old place," she said, gazing about the room in awe as she slid the documents out of the wrappers and placed them on the table, then put her wet basket onto the floor.

Meanwhile, Julia had gone into the kitchen to prepare the tea.

Chapter 20

THE DOCUMENTS

Tim could hardly contain himself as he watched Jessica take her time as she carefully pulled on a pair of surgical gloves before removing the antique sepia photographs and pencil drawings from each individual folder. Then with meticulous movements she methodically arranged the delicate documents in order on the table.

"Are these the original plans and drawings of the old church when it was first built?" he asked, not daring to take his eyes away from what lay before him. Then he felt his heart miss a beat as he looked at a number of faded and wrinkled sepia photographs of not only how the property and its surrounding looked in bygone years, but of the people who had lived there.

"Oh my god," he gasped, standing back from the spread before him.

"I can't believe it."

Tim could hardly tear his eyes away from the image in front of him.

"What is it?" Jessica asked in concern. "Are you alright? Oh my goodness you're Shaking."

"It's nothing," he murmured, apologetically.

Nevertheless, Tim had felt his heart skip a beat when he recognised the emaciated face of Alice, the woman that he and Julia had seen looking in at the window.

Trying not to show the fear he was feeling, Tim pointed to two of the old faded photos.

"Are those of the vicar's wife and his children with the dogs?" he asked.

"I believe so" Jessica replied, "but please don't touch them. Here put these on." Jessica handed him a pair of gloves.

"I always carry extras, because some of the gloves are no good when you remove them from the packet as they are either split or have fingers missing." She explained.

"Anyway, I could hardly believe my eyes when I took a look at what I had bought in the auction. You see, I collect old maps, and I bought this box full at an antique sale in Ripon. But when I got home and emptied the contents of the box onto the table, I was surprised to find these pictures and drawings secreted amongst the maps."

"I didn't know these items were in there, but when I realised they were of the old Church and cottages here at this little village near Laverton. Well, I thought I should keep them as they are of historic value and could be worth something. Besides I am writing a book of history in this area, and I will be including these photos and documents in my book. I did however think, that as you are the new owners of the property it was only right that you should be the first to see them."

Although the drawings on the ancient wrinkled paper were faded, with the help of a magnifying glass on the dotted pencil drawing, Tim felt a surge of excitement race through him when he noticed there was an entrance to a second crypt at a lower level to the first one that appeared at some time to have been bricked up. He wondered why there was no mention of a second crypt on his deeds. However, when he examined one of the old photos through the magnifying glass Tim could hardly conceal his excitement.

"Jessica take a look at this photo," he exclaimed. "James was right, he did see someone watching us when we were at the cottages, and so did the builders." He handed her the photo asking if she could see anyone in the picture.

"I've not really looked that closely," she replied, taking the proffered glass from his hand and taking a closer look.

"Oh my goodness you're right, there is someone there. Wait a minute look further back in the trees." She pointed to an unclear number of individuals who appeared to be standing in the forest as she handed the photo back to him.

Tim took the photo from her trembling fingers to take a closer look at where she Indicated for him to examine the photo in depth.

"Good grief" he exclaimed," the photos are so old and wrinkled that the images of the people are hardly visible I missed them the first time I looked."

He then felt his heart skip a beat as he realised that the blurred image was of a group of people who were partially concealed by the deep foliage. They were standing amongst the bushes and trees gazing up at something that appeared to be two headless men who were strung up and hanging by their feet from two separate thick branches of a tree.

Another wrinkled photo depicted a man dressed in strange clothing, who was stood in front of the trees watching the work being carried out on the old church when it was being developed into cottages.

For a few moments Tim felt a surge of nausea flood through him and he glanced over at Jessica, who by the look on her face, was feeling the same as himself.

Chapter 21

JESSICA

"I'll take a closer look at these when I get home," Jessica said, as she prepared to gather the drawings and photos together.

"I was hoping you would leave them with me," Tim answered hopefully, trying hard to convince her that they were more valuable to him than to her.

"No, sorry, you can copy them on your printer if you wish, but the originals are going home with me" she said as she began putting them together.

Tim almost panicked at the thoughts of her taking the drawings and pictures away, as he had no idea where she lived nor who she really was. He was also afraid that if she left he would never see the valuable documents again.

"No; No;" he exclaimed, trying to keep the panic out of his voice, and grabbed hold of her arm to stop her from replacing them in the plastic folders.

"I'm sorry," he said, releasing his grip on her arm. "I will copy all of them," he said glancing down at the antiquated documentation. "Then it would give me additional time to study them more closely when I'm alone, especially the drawing of the second chamber. I wonder why it wasn't mentioned on the original deeds though." He added rubbing his chin thoughtfully.

It was then that Jessica said something that surprised him.

"If I agree to what you are saying, then would it be possible for you to take me to see the hidden crypt?" she asked hesitantly.

"There must have been a valid reason for it being bricked up, don't you think?"

"I was just thinking that myself" Tim mumbled, surprised by her curiosity at wanting to know the exact area where the crypt was situated.

At that moment Julia arrived and placed the tea tray on the table. "There is sugar and milk if you need it, and biscuits," she said turning towards Jessica. I'll pour the tea and you can help yourself to the milk and sugar."

"Thank you, that is very kind," Jessica said gratefully.

Tim turned to Julia, and was about to say something then stopped, seeing the worried look on her face. In an instant he knew that she had overheard the conversation. "Darling, I know you don't like going down into the basement so would you mind if I took Jessica down?"

"Your husband asked if you would photo copy and scan all of the items here while we take a look below." Jessica interrupted, desperately trying to ease the tension that she could feel growing between the couple.

"There are six pencil drawings, some before the fire and two after. There are also eight photos of the ruined church when it was being turned into cottages in the 1970s.

And photos of the cottages when they were left derelict and the land was covered with overgrown weeds and brambles."

Julia nodded. "You two go, I don't like it down there. Take your time and will do the copying for you."

"Don't forget to put on the gloves, and handle the documents with care because they are very fragile," Jessica said, waggling a podgy finger at her.

Julia grimaced as she picked up the gloves that Jessica had handed to her and pulled them on, she picked up the drawings and photos and took them over to his desk to begin working on them when Tim and Jessica had left the room.

Tim led Jessica along the hall and opened the door leading to the cellar and switched on the light.

"Oh my goodness," Jessica murmured when the brilliant light flooded the whole area. For a few moments she was overcome by the incredible transformation that had been carried out of the property. She stopped momentarily before descending the steps and gazed in awe at the incredible alterations that Tim had carried out. The cellar was now a carpeted games room, with a fitted bar, comfortable chairs and small tables for guests to place their drinks on while relaxing in the pleasant atmosphere, or playing a game of snooker.

She was even more surprised when he opened the second door that led into a fully equipped gymnasium, complete with a television that spanned one wall so he could watch as he exercised, plus a sauna, shower and toilet.

She watched as he moved a screen to one side and felt a flurry of excitement when it revealed a low wooden door.

Tim removed the key from his pocket and unlocked the door, then pushed it open, leant inside, switched on the light and entered the crypt followed by Jessica who was now overcome with excitement.

"Oh my," she gabbled when the light revealed the low arched space and two huge stone ledges on either side of the crypt.

"Is that where they found the bodies?" she asked with a tremor in her voice.

"Yes," Tim replied, "those brown marks on the stone are the blood stains from….."

"Please don't say anymore," she interrupted, turning away from the macabre slabs.

"I think we should concentrate on finding the second tomb. In my estimation the door and passage leading to it should be about there." Jessica pointed to the wall opposite where they had entered.

"You could be right," he replied, indicating towards the ground.

"Look, the stone work here is set on top of the stone flags, while the original flags are abutting the building's structural work. I'll have to get someone in to work on this," he add thoughtfully. "It looks like it could be a big job. Come on, let's get back upstairs to Julia and see how she's getting on with the scanning and copying."

Jessica, who was near to panicking, was relieved by Tim's suggestion of returning to the sanctity of the lounge. She was too afraid to divulge that, as she had been stood waiting for him as he examined the wall, she had noticed the dark shadow of a man standing by the entrance of the crypt. She had also heard the sound of laboured breathing coming from someone whom she couldn't see but who was standing close beside her. But more alarming was the fact that she could feel a child holding her hand.

Nevertheless, Jessica had managed to control her fear, but when they had returned to the lounge she began to wonder if this was the reason why Julia would not enter the cellar.

She did understand though, that whatever was down there was making its presence known and watching every move that she and Tim were making.

Chapter 22

THE CONCEALED CHAMBER

After Jessica had left, Tim contacted James informing him about the photos, documents and drawings regarding the old church and the second chamber. James was overwhelmed, and asked if he could come over right away to see the documents for himself. Tim agreed but he asked James if would be able to organise a team of men as soon as possible to remove the stone blocking the entrance to the chamber.

Within half an hour, James had arrived at the cottage and was asking if he could be there when the concealed chamber was opened. But there was a slight problem he told Tim; when he had contacted the foreman of his work team asking if they would return to the cottage to complete a small job that required urgent attention, the foreman had told James that he would have to find someone else who would be willing to carry out the work, as the men that had worked for him previously on restoring Tim's cottage, didn't want to become involved in any more work at the property.

The ghost sightings and recurring phenomena had been too much for them and no one was happy at the prospect of returning and carrying out the extra duties even though Tim had offered them double wages.

In time James did manage to find four men who agreed to undertake the work, but when the men arrived and saw the rusted blood stains on the slabs where the murdered victims from the past had been concealed, they began having doubts at carrying out the work and huddled together muttering amongst themselves.

Their hesitation and spineless attitude filled Tim with rage.

"It's only a fucking wall," he'd snapped, "all I'm asking is that you remove the stone from in front of an entrance where I presume there will be a locked door. So forget about it, get out. I'll find somebody who can do the job."

Tim's reaction shook the men to the extent that they began to apologise and told him what they had heard about the cottage being haunted. But after Tim had calmed them down he explained to them that no one had been hurt while they were working there, and the men finally agreed to carry out the work.

It took a full day for them to carry out the task of removing the stone barricade without incident. They also took a great deal of care not to damage the floor or the surrounding stone work, and by late afternoon they had uncovered a 5ft high arched solid wooden door behind the stone wall. But as Tim expected, when he tried opening the door he found it to be locked.

Tim was grateful for having the work done, he thanked the men and paid them after they had cleared the excess stone away, then rang James to inform him that the job had been completed. The only problem now was that the door leading into the crypt remained locked.

Tim was frustrated and after a while grumbling to himself he decided to ring James asking if he knew of a reliable locksmith who was capable of dealing with old rusted up antique locks and hinges.

James knew a man who could most likely do the job but he didn't know how busy he was, and told Tim that he would ring him back later as he didn't know the number off hand.

Tim was disappointed when James called back telling him that he would have to wait at least eight days. At the best locksmith he knew, David Haines, had said that as the door had been unused for goodness knows how many years, the lock and hinges would have seized up and the timber would be brittle. Therefore, it could splinter and break if he had to use force.

Tim groaned at the news. He had asked the village locksmith previously, but the man had refused to come anywhere near the cottage, professing that anyone who went near it would be cursed and would receive a cruel death like Old Jake did after he sold it.

Derek Haines, poo pooed the idea of ghosts and curses. The first thing he did when he arrived and went into the crypt was to see for himself how badly the lock and fittings were rusted. He observed that it was stuck solid due to the heavy grease that had been used in the past to ensure that it would open quietly and easily. The grease had thickened and solidified over the years, causing it to set into a solid lump not only on the lock, but on the hinges as well.

Derek was accustomed to these kind of problem's, he moved over to his bag of tools and pulled out the oil he always used for such an occasion. Firstly he sprayed inside the lock then tried numerous old keys before managing to turn the lock. He discovered that the metal hinges of the door had completely deteriorated through lack of use and were covered in rust.

This time he had to use a solvent to soften the rusted metal, then waited for a good half an hour until it began to work. He then used a tool to scratch the excess rust and grime away, then used a sander to grind the remaining rust from the hinges. Derek finally managed to find movement with the door.

He asked Tim to help him by combining both their strength into manoeuvring and manipulating the heavy cast iron studded door until it creaked slowly open, allowing them access onto a stone staircase leading downward that was only visible by the light radiating from behind them.

"It's too dark to go down without a light," Derek said as he peered into the inky blackness. "I can't say for certain but I think there's a passage. Oh what the hell, forget it, I can't see a bloody thing down there."

"Wait a minute," Tim turned and went over to one of the stone slabs where a number of boxes were stacked and began rummaging through them until he found the one he wanted containing a quantity of candles.

"We can use these; I keep them here in case of an emergency," he said, holding them up for Derek to see.

"You take two and I'll have two," he handed the candles over to Derek who took a box of matches from his pocket and lit them.

"Right! Now we can see where we're going."

After ensuring that the five stone steps were safe to stand on, Tim and Derek made their way down until they reached a flagged stairwell, where they found themselves standing in a dark, shrouded, narrow-arched passage leading to another low heavily studded door.

"I hope it isn't locked," Tim groaned, as he took hold of the heavy cast iron loop to open it. To his dismay the door was indeed locked.

"Just a minute," Derek said gruffly, digging his hands into his pocket. "I've got my keys here"

With a bit of a struggle, Derek pulled out a large metal loop holding a number of keys from his pocket and began trying each one, until finally finding one that would fit the door. But again they were frustrated when they found the lock and hinges were completely embedded in rust.

"Don't worry, I'll soon have it sorted," Derek said with a forced laugh, as he turned and hurried back up the stone steps and returned within minutes carrying his trusty bag of tools. Tim held the candles close to Derek as he systematically worked, and using the same procedure as before, and after another hour of struggling, Derek managed to free the lock and hinges allowing the door to creak slowly open.

"Bloody Hell," was all Derek could utter as they backed away from the sickly assortment of fetid odours assaulting their nostrils. For a few moments they hesitated and looked at one another, wary of entering the ominous looking chamber that was completely enveloped by a creepy darkness.

Within seconds of gaining entry they both let out a scream of fear and pain when they were hurled against the wall in the passage behind them by a dark shapeless mass, as it hurtled past them then vanished into the darkness through the thick stone wall alongside them.

"Oh my God, what was that?" Derek whispered hoarsely, grabbing hold of Tim's shoulder in fear that what they had released was going to grab him.

"I don't know," Tim replied shakily, holding up the candle in the hope of guaranteeing the flickering light would bring some prospect of safety.

"But I think the draught could have been caused by us opening the door and ...."

"No it couldn't," snapped Derek who by now was a shaking, quivering, wreck.

"The whole place has been sealed up for centuries and there is nowhere for a draught to come from, because the whole place is dry and air-tight. And another thing, there's no damp down here so those locks and hinges shouldn't have rusted up like they have done."

"Aw shit," Tim cursed loudly when the realisation hit him. The chamber had been sealed to keep something in. But what he wondered."

Derek was sensing that something was now extending into the inhospitable, threatening darkness of the entire area of the crypt. He was terrified of the unknown and glanced nervously from side to side as he held the flickering candles high. He swung them in all direction about himself in an effort to see what could be watching them from the dancing shadows that were being created by the flickering candle's glow.

But when the flame was unexpectedly extinguished they found themselves standing in the inky blackness of the tomb. Derek's sense of danger began to increase until he could stand it no longer. He was anxious to escape from the unseen, unknown entity that was in there with them.

"If you don't mind, I'll be off. I'll leave the key in the lock, you can have it, I've no further use for it" he stammered, and beat a hasty retreat back the way he came.

Leaving the ring of old keys in the door, and Tim alone in the dark confines of the crypt.

It didn't take long for him to follow Derek when he unexpectedly saw a shimmering form appear alongside him. Then to his horror, Tim felt something cold pressing against his body that gave the impression it was pushing onto the bare skin of his arm.

Chapter 23

THE MYSTERIOUS HAND PRINT

In a frenzied panic Tim raced back to the safe confines of his brightly lit office and with trembling hands he poured himself a stiff drink, he then sat in his chair trying to relax.

But no matter how hard Tim tried to unwind he remained tense and fearful of what could happen next. He couldn't let go of the terrible sensation he had felt when some unseen creature had made physical contact with him by touching his face and arm he was still tingling from the nerve-wracking experience.

"I should have worn a jacket or something warmer when I went down there," he mumbled, pulling off his sleeveless sweater to enable him to rub his arm that was beginning to irritate him, then gave a gasp of surprise when seeing a full, raised handprint on the bicep of his arm.

"Oh shit! Julia! Julia," he yelled, leaping to his feet and staring at the awesome sight.

"Come here quick, you've got to see this."

"What now?" she snapped impatiently from the door, "I do have my own work to do."

"Yes I know, I'm sorry, I didn't think," he whispered, "but you have to see this."

Tim half staggered as he moved towards his wife and pulled off his sweater to show her the hand print on his arm.

"What on earth," she gasped when seeing the swollen red welt on his bicep.

"How did you get that? Have you walked into something and not noticed?"

"No," he replied in a wavering voice, "something touched me when I was with Derek in the second chamber, the crypt, the tomb, whatever you want to call it."

Julia noticed that his voice was reaching a level of hysteria when he began striding about the room.

"Tim, sit down and talk to me and explain what happened when you were with the locksmith," she commanded.

Tim stopped pacing the room and seated himself in the armchair, where much to Julia's annoyance he began drumming his fingers on the chair arm.

"We were in the chamber, the crypt," he started to explain. "When all of a sudden something happened and Derek ran out screaming and left me on my own.

"What chamber? What crypt? what are you talking about?"

"The chamber in the drawing that Jessica brought, the second crypt."

"Oh my God, you didn't go searching for that did you?"

"Yes I did, and thankfully Derek was with me"

"So! What did you find? Where is he?"

"You mean what didn't we find? The bloody coward turned tail and ran when we opened the second door. We both saw and felt a dark mass rush past us that threw us against the passage wall then disappeared through the wall alongside of us, that's when he ran. He left me on my own, then something cold touched me. To be honest it freaked me out so I ran."

"Come into the kitchen, that swelling looks nasty, I'll bathe it and put a dressing on."

Tim was about to do as Julia suggested then he had a thought.

"Just a minute I want James to see this before we do anything, perhaps he can offer an explanation as to what it could mean."

Tim took his mobile from his pocket and called James telling him that he wanted to see him. He urgently needed to show him something of vital importance, and would explain everything in detail when he arrived.

It didn't take long for James curiosity to leap into high gear, he wanted to know more about the concealed chamber and readily agreed to come and hear what Tim had to say.

For a full half an hour Tim waited impatiently for James to arrive, while Julia went into the kitchen to prepare a cold compress for his throbbing arm. Meanwhile, James arrived promptly within the expected half hour and had hardly got through the door before he began asking questions.

Chapter 24

THE CHALLENGE

"Alright, let's hear it," James demanded to know picking up a ham sandwich from the plate Julia had placed on the table. "And what's that cloth doing on your arm?" he asked pointing to the cold compress.

Tim looked directly into James clear blue eyes and watched his facial expressions change when he told him what had occurred in the chamber. He then lifted the cloth to show him the raised welt of a hand impression on his arm.

"Good grief," he exclaimed in awe. "Are you sure you two haven't been fighting?" he remarking jokingly. "I thought you were too old for that."

Tim was furious' he didn't have time for bantering.

"I felt that you had to see this for yourself' Tim snapped angrily, leaping to his feet.

"But if you've not got anything better to say then you can fuck off, I shouldn't have rung you."

James instantly realised that he had said the wrong thing and that Tim's nerves were truly shredded and he was almost at breaking point.

"Come on man, I was only joking," he said trying to make light of the situation and put his around Tim's shoulder. But Tim shrugged him off.

"Joking or not," Tim snapped, "Forget it, I should never have called you, I think you should leave."

Julia was as surprised as James by Tim's bitter comments. let me get us all a drink to soothe our nerves," she suggested loudly to overcome the sound of Tim's angry voice, and went over to the drink's cabinet to pour them a tumbler filled with whiskey and handed it to them.

"Then when we have all calmed down," she said between sips of cognac, "Tim can explain in detail what happened."

"I'm sorry, I didn't mean what I just said, I was only joking," James apologised once more.

Tim's voice was sombre as he spoke, "Apology accepted, but don't make stupid remarks like that again. Right."

"Right," James said glancing at Julia, who rolled her eyes and said nothing.

"Okay" James broke the ice, "what happened that you said was of vital importance for me to see?"

Tim began to relate in detail everything that he and Derek had experienced in the chamber, including the glowing phantom figure that had touched his face and arm. He then unwrapped and removed the cold compress to show Jason the bizarre hand print.

"Bloody hell" James remarked softly as he examined the strange blemish on his friend's arm. "Do you think it was at all possible for you to have accidentally brushed against something bearing the resemblance of a hand?" he asked. "You said yourself that you couldn't see a thing because it was so dark in there."

"No," Tim replied, he was adamant about what he and Derek had encountered when opening the door to the chamber.

James listened intently to what Tim was saying and unexpectedly felt a trickle of fear sweep through him. When thinking about the vicar who slaughtered his entire family and the dogs, then stored their bleeding corpses in the crypt next door to the newly discovered chamber his blood ran cold.

'Could it have been the ghost of Alice, the mother of murdered children, that Tim had seen standing beside him and felt her touch him as he stood alone in the flickering candlelight he wondered? Or was it a figment of his over-active imagination while being alone in the dismal crypt with only the memories of the dead for companionship.

"Oh my God, look," Julia suddenly cried, disrupting James; thoughts.

"Tim, look at your arm."

They all stared in amazement as the hand print began to fade before completely disappearing from Tim's arm and leaving no trace of it ever having been there.

James was in a spin, "What the devil," he murmured softly then grabbed hold of Tim as his knees began to buckle beneath him and he seated him in the armchair. Julia tried to control the panic that was welling inside her as she moved to Tim's side and raised his arm so that she and James could clearly see, the now unblemished skin.

"Whatever caused the curious welt wanted you to see it James." Julia's voice trembled as she spoke.

"I think you're right," he admitted, shaking his head in confusion. For a few moments a silence descended before James finally spoke.

"After giving the matter some thought," he said in a controlled tone, "I think we ought to go back and investigate that chamber Tim, it is my belief that something in there is trying to make contact with you."

Tim could hardly believe what he was hearing.

"You have to be joking," he stuttered incredulously, staring at James with a stunned expression on his face.

"No, I'm not, I mean it Tim. Something in there is definitely trying to reach you, and when it does, then maybe it will enable us to clear up the mystery of the hauntings in the cottage and the surrounding woods."

Tim was scared to death at the thought of returning to the chamber.

Chapter 25

THE PASSAGE

Despite Julia's warnings Tim had finally relented and agreed to go with James and show him the chamber. Upon reaching the basement door Tim had turned and asked James if he was certain that he wanted to proceed any further.

"Of course I do," he replied.

Tim, noticed that there was a slight hesitancy in James' manner when he switched on the light and opened the door leading down into the basement.

As they began descending the cellar steps, James unexpectedly grabbed hold of Tim's sweater to stop him from proceeding any further.

"Shush," James held up his hand indicating for Tim to be silent. "Listen."

"What?" Tim whispered.

"Can't you hear it?"

"Hear what?"

"Shit, it's stopped, I distinctly heard the sound of women's voices, they were talking to one another."

Tim froze for a moment and stared about the newly fitted-out games room but couldn't see anything out of place.

"What were they saying?" he asked hesitantly keeping his voice low.

"I couldn't make it out" James whispered. "Didn't you hear them?"

"No," Tim replied. He stood for a few moments listening intently for any sounds other than the echoes of thunder from the raging storm outside.

"It could have been the thunder or the rain that you were hearing, the storm is pretty bad right now."

"You could be right," James replied, then gave a shrug and carried on following Tim.

As they entered the first crypt he stopped and pointed to the rusty brown stains on the stone slabs on either side of the first chamber.

"Why are those marks still on the stone?" he asked, "I thought you'd had the place cleaned up when you first moved in."

"I did, but no amount of scrubbing can remove those stains. When we do try to erase them they're back within the hour. I was told by Rose Oldsworthy at the pub, that they were the bloodstains of the vicar's wife and children that he had slaughtered, and hidden down here. She said that it's part of the curse and nothing can be done to remove the stains from the blood bath that occurred here."

James felt his stomach churn "Bloody hell," he muttered, unable to think of anything other to say.

"Come on," Tim gave James a prod to get him moving and pointed to a cluster of old candles and oil lamps standing on one of the stone slabs.

"I always keep the candles and a box of matches here, and these lamps full of oil just in case the power goes off, so we'd better light them then we can get moving."

Tim's hands were shaking as he lit two of the oil lamps and handed them to James before lighting two for himself.

"We only need one each don't we?"

"No" Tim snapped impatiently, "if one goes out then we each have a spare I told you, its dark in there."

Without saying another word Tim opened the now unconcealed door, that led through a narrow passage towards another low-arched doorway. Due to both men being so tall they had to stoop to go through the door that opened onto a narrow flight of five stone steps.

"Flaming hell, look at the cobwebs. This place hasn't been used for years and it stinks," James kept his voice low as if expecting someone to overhear what he was saying. Tim ignored him and held the lamp as high as he could before cautiously making his way down the stone steps and into the narrow passage that was eerily silent.

"Ouch! Shit, I didn't expect it to be this low," James grumbled, rubbing his head when banging it on the low stone arched roof. He bent his six feet frame even lower to enable him to move forward. As he did so James suddenly felt a sense of unease.

He put a hand on Tim's shoulder causing Tim to jump and yell in fear.

"What the hell are you playing at you silly bugger" he snapped feeling his whole being shaking with fear.

"I think there is somebody behind me, can you take a look? I can't bear to see what it is," he croaked.

"For goodness sake man," Tim hissed, turning the top half of his body to look behind them, but James hulking shoulders and the darkness behind them was blocking him from seeing any further than James himself.

"I can't see anything," Tim lied. James let out a sigh of relief, but he shuddered when he felt the cold hard stone as it brushed against his wide shoulders which were almost touching the walls of the confined space they were struggling through.

"I did tell you it was a tight squeeze," Tim mumbled, who was equally uncomfortable in their surroundings. Nevertheless, it was only a few yards they had to shuffle before reaching the closed door to the chamber.

Chapter 26

JAMES INSIDE THE BURIAL CHAMBER

"Have you been inside?" James asked not daring to take his eyes away from the door.

"No' I've only partially opened it with Derek and that was enough. We weren't prepared for anything bad happening, and we only had candle light so everything was in darkness. When that thing shot past us it scared the living daylights out of us both."

"What thing?"

"How the hell should I know what it was. All we saw was a dark shadow," Tim responded icily. "As it sped past we were flung against the wall then it disappeared through that wall over there."

"Oh shit!" James groaned, when seeing how narrow the passage was. "What if it's still here," he quivered.

Tim ignored him and carried on speaking, "It scared the hell out of me when Derek panicked and ran. Then that other shape appeared and touched me, so I didn't wait to find out what it was I slammed the door shut and locked it and got the hell out of here."

Tim could see the stricken look of apprehension on James' face.

"If you don't want to take it any further then we can go back upstairs," he offered.

Tim himself wasn't too happy at the thought of entering the chamber, as he was concerned about what they would find in there.

Nevertheless James couldn't mistake the fear in Tim's voice, and putting on a false bravado he forced himself to encourage Tim to go forward, indicating for him to open the door and enter the chamber. Within seconds, James felt his heart lurch when Tim turned the key that Derek had left behind in the lock in his frantic effort to escape the ungodly spectre floating around them, and pushed the door open.

"Oh my god," he murmured, feeling his mouth suddenly becoming dry with fear.

The light from their lamps sent weird shadows cascading about the interior of the chamber. "I don't believe it," he gasped, when the light from Tim's lantern broke through the inky blackness encompassing the chamber.

Tim was equally shocked when they entered the twenty foot wide eight feet high circular, domed room and stood staring open mouthed at the incredible contents.

James almost dropped the lamp with shock, when the light lit up the sculpted figure of a menacing, gigantic, armoured Knight Templar. The warrior appeared to have been carved from one complete block of marble that was fixed to the centre of the curved wall in the domed room. He was attired in a full suit of body armour and held a huge broadsword in front of himself, while a large hunting hound lay at his feet. The full area surrounding him bore the insignia of the knights Templar cross. But the eeriest of all were his piercing cold stone eyes that seemed to bore deep into the depths of anyone looking at him.

It was obvious that the statue had been built into the wall at the same time as the chamber was being erected; feet were firmly embedded in the ground and his helmet was touching the ceiling where large blocks of stone abutted the figure.

The carving was so lifelike it struck fear into the heart of anyone seeing it.

After overcoming the initial shock, Tim warily lifted both his lamps and peered about in the darkness until he spotted a huge marble sarcophagus. It was set alongside of the wall that was bearing the effigy of a woman whose likeness was carved in white marble.

"Oh my," he whispered in awe, and moved cautiously forward towards it while calling for James to come and take a look at what he had found.

James was oblivious to where Tim was indicating, because at that moment he was looking in the opposite direction. When the fluctuating light from his flickering lamps fell upon the most horrendous and gruesome sight that anyone could ever imagine.

The only sound emanating from James was the choking gasp of breath as it escaped from his paralysed throat. When the oscillating light from his lamps fell upon three mummified women who were dressed in long silken robes. The material was now faded and had partially disintegrated over the years revealing the skeletal bone structure of each woman. The remains that had lain there, undisturbed, for over a hundred years, were seated on three exotically carved stone thrones bearing an inverted cross of Christ above their heads.

Each mummified woman had been secured in place by a number of narrow chains that were surrounding their bodies and were facing the marble sarcophagus.

"Oh no," James murmured softly, and cringed as he took in the gruesome sight of their wizened skin pulled taut across their sunken, hollow eye sockets and yellowed skulls. The remaining tufts of hair contributed to their hideous appearance.

The once colourful silken clothing was now faded and ragged, draped around their shrunken bodies but unbelievably, still intact, as were the sequined shoes on their shrivelled feet.

At first, James could hardly believe what he was looking at and held up his lamp to get a closer view, then shrieked when sensing that the corpses were watching and grinning at him.

"Come on James, we're getting out of here" Tim yelled, grabbing hold of James' arm and began pulling. James however was oblivious to everything other than the hideous corpses that held him in a state of suspended animation.

"Come on James," Tim shouted yanking him hard, then stopped when a foul stink began filling the entire chamber.

"James, we've got to get out of here. Now I understand why this place was sealed."

Still James didn't move.

"For God's sake man, come on."

Tim felt a surge of panic when grasping the dire situation they had placed themselves in, and although he didn't want to do it, Tim balled his hand into a fist and landed a heavy blow to the side of James head, causing James to reel when the unanticipated clout pulled him out of his stunned state.

"James, we've got to get out of this godforsaken place now before it's too late."

James didn't answer because he was so shocked by the blow but he allowed Tim to guid him towards the open doorway. Tim was shaking with fright at what might happen next but managed to push James out from the oppressive death chamber then slammed the door shut and locked it firmly behind them.

He slipped the key into his pocket, propelled James ahead of him through the short corridor, up the steps and out through the door at the top of the stairs then locked it. He extinguished the lamps and placed them on the stone slab. When that was done both men hurried through the first chamber, through the gym and games room and quickly made their way back up to Tim's office.

Chapter 27

JULIA

Unbeknown to them, at the time they entered the chamber Julia had been upstairs in the spare room and had just walked out onto the landing, when the lights began to flicker and dim.

"Oh no," she groaned, when hearing a loud clatter of thunder "I hope the storm isn't going to affect the lights."

Julia's body tensed when the lights suddenly faded and she was engulfed in darkness. "Oh no;" she cried again and retreated backwards, glancing fearfully around.

In rapid succession, brilliant flashes of lightning lit up the entire hallway below, casting unearthly shadows and illuminating the form of someone lurking in the dark recess of the doorway.

Julia could feel her whole body become rigid with fear and was almost in tears. Then came an added shock, when for a brief moment, she noticed the faint outline of a man standing on the landing only a few feet away from her.

"Oh my god, Tim, where are you? she cried silently. Her nerves were totally on edge with what had occurred in the cottage a few days ago, and now this was happening.

"Please, please God, don't let anything come near me," she pleaded as she waited anxiously in the gloomy atmosphere, hearing the loud rumbles of thunder passing overhead.

As if her prayers had been answered the generator that Tim had had fitted for such an emergency kicked in and the light was restored.

Julia clutched her hands to her chest, and felt a sense of overwhelming relief flood through her. But just as she was just about to go down the stairs she stopped, as a beautiful, elegantly dressed woman drifted up the stairs towards her.

"How did you get in? The doors are locked" Julia's voice was almost a whisper as she spoke.

The woman didn't reply but kept slowly moving up the staircase towards her.

Although she was terrified, Julia noticed that the woman was clad in a full length ivory coloured silk dress trimmed with lace and matching gloves that reached to her elbows.

On her blonde, perfectly coiffured hair she wore a hat with a co-ordinating lace trim to blend with her dress. At a guess Julia could only surmise that she was adorned in the style of the late 1700 or early 1800s.

For a few moments Julia gazed in awe at the incredible sight before experiencing a bolt of fear as she observed that the woman was not walking up the staircase, she was floating.

Julia felt as if a cold hand was grasping her heart; it was pounding so fast and loud that she could hear it throbbing as the blood pulsated through her ears.

Her throat had become dry leaving her unable to utter a sound.

She could only watch, stupefied with shock and petrified with fear, as the ghostly apparition made its way slowly towards her.

The sight of the spectral figure threw Julia's mind into a chaotic mess; she couldn't think straight nor could she call out for help. She slowly backed away along the landing until she could go no further when feeling herself bump into something behind her.

Julia hardly dare take her eyes away from the vision of the woman as she drew closer, but as she approached, the ghostly apparition unexpectedly lifted her arm and pointed directly towards something at the back of her.

Julia, was afraid of seeing what was blocking her way of escape into one of the bedrooms. But when she did manage to pull her gaze away from the approaching phantom Julia turned her head she let out a piercing scream as she saw two headless, male corpses standing close behind her.

In a fraction of a second sheer terror encompassed her entire being and she couldn't move and froze with fear as her mind slowly absorbed the macabre sight of the two decapitated men.

Then as quickly as all three apparitions had appeared they were gone. The spectral woman and the two hideous, headless corpses had evaporated into empty space, leaving.

Julia lying semi-conscious on the carpeted balcony.

For a short time Julia couldn't move at all, she lay there and prayed that the apparitions were gone and that she would soon have the strength to get to her feet and call Tim. It wasn't to be. Suddenly a tremendous pain exploded in her chest and she felt the strength draining from her body, then total darkness engulfed her.

Chapter 28

DEATH

As James and Tim stumbled into the office, Tim suddenly sensed that something was wrong and called to his wife. When Julia didn't reply he went into the kitchen to see if she was there, but was surprised to find it empty.

Alarmed, he asked James to search one side of the cottage while he searched the other, but after repeatedly calling her name he still got no response. It was then Tim remembered that she was going upstairs to tidy the bedroom then sort through some things that had yet to be unpacked.

"Come on James, she must be upstairs in one of the spare rooms"

Concerned, at the lack of response from Julia, they made their way up the staircase but when they reached the landing Tim was shocked to see his wife lying unconscious with a terrified look on her face.

"Julia," he called, racing to her side and kneeling beside her.

"James;" he yelled, "help me; what do we do?" he screamed in panic.

James hurried to his side and knelt down beside Julia to check her pulse.

"Come on, Tim, help me lift her onto the bed where she will be more comfortable."

James didn't say anything to Tim as they placed her on the bed, but when he had checked Julia's pulse as she lay on the floor, he had found that her heart had stopped beating. Julia was dead.

"Tim, ring for an ambulance while I try to ger her heart going again."

Tim nodded and mumbled something incoherent, and fumbled in his pocket for his mobile, but it wasn't there.

"Damn," he cursed, when realising that he must have dropped it when they were fleeing to escape from the chamber.

He threw a stricken glance towards James then raced down the stairs where he called the emergency services from the house phone.

James, meanwhile, had loosened Julia's clothing and began CPR attempting to breathe air into her lungs. When the medics arrived it was too late, there was nothing anyone could do to bring her round.

The medic said that she must have had a massive heart attack and died immediately, but from the look of sheer terror on Julia's face they deduced something terrible must have happened, as she appeared to have been frightened to death.

Chapter 29

RUPERT

Tim felt tense and uneasy about the children coming home for their mother's funeral. He never expected Annabella to be so overwhelmed with grief that she was inconsolable and had to be sedated. It was the doctor's recommendation that she should stay at home and be put to bed as she was not fit enough to attend the service, especially the burial.

It was noticeable however, throughout the service that Rupert was desperately trying to control his emotions and keep a stiff upper lip. He couldn't hold back the tears as the funeral service progressed, and sobbed openly as he read the ellogy in memory of his mother. Then with his father and many others, he completely broke down when her casket was taken outside and prayers were said over her as they finally lowered it into the ground, knowing they would never see or touch her ever again.

Surviving the Wake was another terrible ordeal. An open buffet was held at a nearby hotel, where guests offered their condolences and offers of help should Tim need it. He knew they had been Julia's friends and he would never see or hear from them again, and he was only too pleased when the last guest left and he could go home to check on Annabella.

Francesca, who was Tim's younger sister had stayed behind to take care of Annabella while the funeral had taken place. Afterwards she had asked the children if they wanted to go and stay with her until their father had sold the cottage. Annabella had quickly agreed to go as she believed the cottage had been the cause of her mother's death and hated it.

Rupert said that he would stay until his break was over and then he would return to camp and carry on with his training. He had insisted that before he left his father should take him into the newly discovered chamber.

Tim went ballistic; he would not agree to taking Rupert anywhere near it.

"For your own safety, and for the safety of the rest of us, I don't believe it would be wise to take you there," he told his son.

"James was ill for a week after what we saw in there. Then after what happened to your mother." Tim lowered his head as he tried unsuccessfully to fight back the tears.

"We don't want any more problems, so no, you can't go in there."

"But dad, I am almost nineteen years old," Rupert argued.

"No buts', and that's final," Tim's voice was firm. "You are not going down there, James and I believe that your mother's death was somehow linked to what happened when we opened that chamber. So no, you are not to go anywhere near it, and besides you will need these to get in."

Tim took the keys from his pocket and dangled them in front of his son.

"I will not give them to you, so you can forget about it."

Rupert stood clenching his fists and glared angrily at his father as Tim put the keys back into his pocket.

"By the way," Tim spoke in a softer tone in an effort to break the tension that had built between them, and placed a comforting hand on Rupert's shoulder.

"I understand how you feel, but you have to take into consideration my feelings as well; I loved your mother more than you will ever know." Tim took a few moments to control the emotion that was building inside him.

"I have asked our friend, David Hartley, the priest from St George's Church, to come and bless the cottage and both chambers. It may be possible for him to could carry out an exorcism after he sees what is in the Crypt, otherwise he may decide that he needs a higher authority to help with the exorcism. I will be honest with you Rupert, James and I do believe that entering that chamber had something to do with your mother's death."

"Now can we leave it at that until David has been."

"Alright dad but on one condition."

'Oh God, what now? Tim thought' knowing what was coming.

"I want to come with you and David to see for myself what is in that chamber, and try to work out the reason, and understand what happened to my mother."

"Let me think about it son."

"No, I'm coming with you. For goodness, sake, I am not a child." Rupert shouted at his dad.

"Rupert, I don't want anything to happen to you like it did to your mother." Tim responded angrily. "For Heaven's sake, don't let us argue like this, not today. Not when we have just buried your mother."

Rupert lowered his head so that his father couldn't see the tears that were threatening to fall, and felt ashamed of himself for his outburst.

"If you believe that mum saw a ghost that frightened her to death, then I want to know who the ghost was," he mumbled.

"Son."

"No Dad" Rupert implored holding up his hands in frustration, "I'm not afraid of ghosts. They say the college is haunted where I am studying. Books and other objects have been moved when no-one is standing near them, and weird shadows of people have been seen at night in the Mess Hall that disappear as soon they are aware they have been noticed. So one night three of us got together and waited in there for something to happen, but when it did two of the lads chickened out and ran. After that nothing has been seen. We've even gone outside at midnight but we haven't noticed anything but the odd fox and rabbit. So as I say, I am not afraid of the dark nor of ghosts."

"Alright, alright," Tim held his hands up in defeat.

"But I can promise you this, it is not a pretty sight and you must swear that you will never disclose to anyone what you see down there."

For a few moments Rupert looked at his father, puzzled by his words, but from the serious look on his father's face Rupert began to realise that it must have been something horrific to have caused the turmoil that his dad and James had experienced when they were in the chamber.

As Rupert stood looking at his father, a muddle of thoughts began whirling around in his head about what was in the chamber.

Why had it been sealed and bricked up so many centuries ago? What lay shrouded behind the stone wall? Why had its whereabouts been kept secret and unknown for so long?

Chapter 30

THE PRIEST DAVID HARTLEY

When David arrived at the cottage he took two steps back before opening the gate, sensing something was wrong. He couldn't quit put his finger on it, but whatever it was, it was attempting to stop him from entering the property. Despite his qualms he mumbled a prayer of protection before opening the wrought iron gate and making his way along the path towards the cottage.

But before reaching the door he recoiled in horror as he saw Julia standing there with a hideous grin on her face waiting to greet him.

"Oh God" he whispered, "what's happening here? I was at the funeral when they buried her."

"David, hello, come in, come in," David was startled out of his shocked stupor when he heard Tim's voice and saw him standing alone in the open doorway.

"Where is she?" he stammered, "Julia I've just seen her."

"What? You can't have, she's dead. You were there when we buried her in your parish cemetery."

"No, I tell you she was stood exactly where you are standing right now."

Tim stared at David in disbelief and felt a cold shudder run through him.

"Oh bloody hell," he mumbled and then it came out in a jumbled mass of words.

"I think we'd better get inside," Tim said as he quickly scanned outside before pulling David into the hall and closing the door behind him.

David had felt unnerved by the unnatural look on Julia's, face, and hesitantly followed Tim into the lounge, glancing around, aware that something was amiss in the cottage. He was stunned by the revelation that he had just seen Julia's ghost.

"Here, I think you need this, and sit down." Tim's voice echoed around his confused thoughts, as he felt Tim nudging him towards the armchair handing him a large tumbler full of whiskey.

"Thanks, I need it," David acknowledged as he seated himself taking a large gulp of the proffered drink. "What the devil's going on here?" he asked after he had managed to calm himself.

"You said you saw Julia?" Tim's face was ashen as he spoke and he felt stupid asking the question as soon as he had said it.

"Yes, she was standing at the door, then she disappeared."

"Are you certain it was Julia?"

"Of course I'm certain, you know me well enough to understand that I am not in the habit of concocting such a stupid statement like that."

"I'm sorry David, but you must admit that it was a bit of a shock hearing what you've just said."

"Think of what it was like for me seeing her standing there and looking as normal as you and me. Now let's change the subject" David glanced warily about the room, but he didn't dare mention the hideous smirk that had crossed Julia's face when she met him at the door.

"What was it that you wanted to speak to me about that you couldn't tell me over the phone?" David asked, desperately trying to stay focuss on the reason why he had been asked to come to the cottage so soon after the funeral.

By the time Tim had explained everything to him, David was ready for his glass to be refilled.

"If it's as bad as you say," he commented thoughtfully, "then I think I am going to be needing help from a higher authority. First you will have to take me to the chamber to see for myself what is in there, then I will be prepared for whatever I will be dealing with."

"For a start, you will be needing all the faith you can muster," Tim warned, "and you must be prepared for the worst."

Chapter 31

DAVID IN THE CHAMBER

Tim led the way and was about to enter the basement, when he heard Rupert calling.

"Oh shit," he muttered softly so David didn't hear and pressed the light switch then pushed David through the door onto the first level of the steps and locked the door behind them.

David, however, hesitated for a few moments on the ledge at the top of the steps and although he couldn't see anything, he sensed that someone was moving about in the room below.

"Are we alone here?" he asked, feeling slightly uncomfortable as he looked down into the well-lit and spacious games room.

"Yes," Tim replied. "Why?"

"Because I feel as if I am descending into an impenetrable dark void of evil." David replied, moving slowly forward and counting each step down until he was standing on the carpeted floor. He waited for a few moments and glanced uneasily about taking in his surroundings before taking a few deep breaths and moving forward. He crossed himself uttered a few quiet prayers, then stopped.

"What is it, have you sensed something?" Tim asked in concern.

"It must be my imagination," he said, turning to face Tim.

"What do you mean?" Tim was surprised by the way his friend was reacting.

"Nothing really," David shrugged, embarrassed by his own nervous response.

"I'm afraid with all the myths and tales I have heard and read about this place, I believe they're starting to get to me."

Tim pretended that he hadn't noticed the sharpness in David's tone and tried to act as normally as possible as he led him from the games room then through the gymnasium. He moved the screen to one side revealing the door to the first crypt, which he unlocked and opened then led David through.

"Before you ask," Tim's voice suddenly interrupted his thoughts, "those brown marks on the stones are blood stains from the vicar's victims, and are impossible to remove. And the door you can see opposite where we are standing, is where we are going."

Immediately, David sensed the tension within Tim, and was about to say something, when Tim suddenly continued speaking.

"Once we are through that door, there are three steps down that lead along a short, low, narrow passage to the second chamber so watch your head. Then there is another door that like the others that is kept locked. So are you ready?

"Ready as I'll ever be," David replied softly, wondering what could be so alarming that it was causing Tim's strange behaviour. He had known Tim and Julia for a number of years and they had become good friends. They had attended his church on a weekly basis and visited one-another's homes regularly. In that time Tim had never acted in as an odd a manner as he was doing now. David began to wonder if it was the death of Julia that was affecting him.

At this crucial moment however, he didn't want to distress Tim any further by asking awkward questions. He stood watching as Tim plugged in the industrial electric lamp he used for his work then switched it on.

"Here we go," Tim said, giving David a quick glance then turned his attention back to the door. The instant he unlocked the door and pushed it open, the dense murky darkness in the passage was illuminated by the brilliant radiance of the light, revealing the steps leading down to an ancient stone passage and the to the mysterious chamber beyond.

David felt his heart race at what he was about to see, and although he was a big man with strong religious beliefs, he felt a tremor of fear race through him and found himself clutching his bible with one hand while with the other hand, he firmly gripped the cross firmly that he always wore around his neck. He followed Tim who stopped when reaching the door and turned towards him.

"Are you certain you want to see this? I can confirm that only James and I have been in there and I promise you, it is not for the faint-hearted, it is pretty gruesome."

David nodded his head acknowledging Tim's question. He had seen plenty of horrendous sights in his time, but nothing had prepared him for what he was about to encounter when stepped into this chamber of horrors.

Chapter 32

DAVID

"Oh my God," David gasped, dropping to his knees and crossing himself while at the same time holding high the cross that he was carrying. He prayed when the light lit up the three mummified figures facing the carved marble sarcophagus set alongside the wall opposite.

"Get up man, praying isn't going to do them any good now." Tim snapped, pulling David to his feet.

"Have you informed the authorities?" David's words came out in a garbled mumble.

"No," Tim spoke sharply. "I wanted you to see it first before I did anything, if the press gets hold of this then all hell will break loose and there will be no stopping them.

What we have found here will make news headlines around the world, then I won't be able to sell the cottage. You know as well as I do that nobody wants to live in a house where mass murders have been committed, let alone this." Tim swung out his arms barely able to look at the sickening carnage surrounding him.

"This had to be murder nobody in their right minds would have come and sat here and waited to die, look at the positions of the bodies," David pointed out.

David had to force himself to move closer to get a better look at the three shrivelled corpses.

"If all three had died a natural death they wouldn't be seated here like this, they would have been contorted." He said pointing to the upright bodies.

"Good grief, may God have mercy on their souls," he murmured softly.

"Tim, come closer," he whispered in a barely audible voice.

"What is it? Tim moved to his side trying hard not to look at the grotesque figures.

"If you look closely," he pointed to separate areas of the bodies, "you will see that there are three lengths of chain around each corpse. One round the neck, one round the waist and the other across its chest supporting it in an upright position. Each chain is secured by separate hooks that have been driven into the stone." He stood back rubbing his chin as he stared thoughtfully, wondering, at the meticulous planning that had gone into securing the corpse's.

It's my opinion" he stated, "that these three women were killed then dressed and seated here. Whoever put the women here had it all pre-planned."

David turned to face Tim. "We must report our findings to the proper authorities, then I will arrange for these poor creatures to have a proper Christian burial."

Tim could hardly believe what David was saying. "Hang on a minute, I was hoping that you would carry out an exorcism in here, then we could reseal the room and brick the door up and forget about it."

"Tim, you can't just do that." David argued, "someone, somewhere has to be the descendants of these people. He turned back to take another look at the corpses and let his gaze drop to the skeletal hands, where he observed an obscure design on a ring on the bony finger of one of the mummies.

"Oh my God," he whispered, "Tim."

David turned to point out the inscriptions on the ring but when he looked around Tim was nowhere in sight. He stifled a groan when he looked over to the opposite side of the chamber and saw that Tim was on his knees busy rubbing at the words inscribed on the woman's marble sarcophagus.

"Have you found something?" David asked, peering into the shadows behind the sarcophagus.

"Yes," Tim replied enthusiastically, "this woman's name was Angela Von something or other of Leon, France." He straightened up looking directly at David.

"Someone, at some-time or another, has attempted to eradicate her name, date of birth and death from the sarcophagus by partially chiselling them away.

"You can't be serious."

"I am, and that means somebody has been in the crypt before us. Somebody who knew her and was pissed off with her and has tried to eliminate all knowledge of her existence."

"But who in their right mind would do a thing like that?"

"I don't know," Tim replied, maybe it was the person who sealed up the chamber.

Whoever did this had to have a really big grievance against these women."

"Yes, I believe so, and if you notice the marks on the floor, they show that another sarcophagus was here but it's been removed. For what reason? And why? We don't know. Tim do you realise this isn't just a crypt? I believe it was meant to be a family vault."

"You could be right," Tim said as he acknowledged David's theory with a nod of his head.

"Now, would you come and see what I've discovered," David said in serious tone.

Chapter 33

THE RING

David led Tim over to the three mummified women and pointed to their skeletal fingers.

"Look, at the rings all three cadavers are wearing; rings bearing an identical insignia.

It's my guess that these women were killed and mummified because they were involved in some kind of ritual magic. Whoever is in that sarcophagus was involved as well."

He had gained Tim's attention in seconds. "The rings are bearing an ancient runic symbol and in my opinion," David's voice was filled with excitement as he explained with a flourish of enthusiasm, "these women were killed and placed here as either a punishment or to guard their mistress following her death, and to guard her against evil spirits."

"Go on," Tim could hardly conceal the eagerness in his voice, anxious to hear more of what David had to say.

"I can't see any other logical explanation for the corpses to have been chained to those thrones." David added. "Those mummified bodies have been placed there for a specific reason, but what, I can't say for certain. But, I really do believe that as I said previously, we should inform the police as soon as possible about what we have discovered here."

"Of course you are right, but first do you think we could take a closer look at one of those rings to see if we can find out what those strange carvings are?"

"Oh yes, it's as easy as that." David replied glancing down at the long bony fingers. and felt his stomach churn at the thought of touching them.

"Why don't you do it, after all, I am a man of the cloth and if I were to touch it then it would mean I would be desecrating a corpse."

He looked at Tim and saw that he was equally as squeamish at the thought of carrying out such a gruesome task.

"I'll tell you what," David said reluctantly, "If I held the hand then could you remove the ring without pulling the finger off as you pull it over the bones?"

"Me?" Tim uttered in dismay. He was repulsed at the idea of touching a corpse that had been dead for hundreds of years, let alone removing a ring from a bony finger that could break apart immediately it was touched.

"You want me to do it." he said backing away.

"Well, it was your idea in the first place," David responded, angry at Tim and his bright idea.

" You were never squeamish at school in the lab when we had to dissect live animals."

"That was different he stammered."

"Now if you don't mind I would like to get out of here, so are we going to take the ring as you suggested or not?"

"Oh for goodness sake," Tim grumbled. Reluctantly, he pulled his handkerchief from his pants pocket to protect his fingers from touching the bones of the skeletal hand.

He grimaced as he set about removing the ring from the bony finger. Things however didn't go as they planned when the finger came away with the ring and Tim was left holding the grotesque object in his hand.

"Oh shit," he yelled, throwing the finger to one side where it bounced off David's face.

"What the hell are you doing?" David shrieked jumping to his feet and dashing the object away from his head. "Now look what you've made me do." By now he was hysterical when he saw that he was holding the mummy's arm in his hand. Screaming, he dropped the arm onto the floor.

"What do we do? "What do we do?" He yelled, leaping about in alarm and pointing to the detached hand and arm lying on the ground.

"I don't fucking know," Tim shouted. "Let's get out of here."

"We can't," David retorted, "someone will know we've been in here. We can't just leave those bits lying there."

"We can, let them think the rats have done it."

"Don't talk so bloody stupid," David retorted angrily. "Tim, we have to try to refix that arm and hand otherwise the first person who see them will notice there is a ring missing, and you will be accused of grave robbing."

For a short while Tim stood staring at the bones lying on the floor, feeling ill at the thought of trying to reattach them to the corpse.

"You're right" he said after a while, "we can't just leave them lying there, but I have another suggestion."

"Oh boy, here we go again," David muttered to himself. He was fast running out of patience with Tim and looked doubtfully at him, waiting to hear what daft idea he had thought up now.

"Alright, what is it?" he asked in a belligerent tone.

"Do you think we could leave them on the floor? If we kick them closer to the mummy then maybe it will appear they dropped off naturally."

"That's a daft idea," David snapped. "Oh God" he moaned softly, grabbing hold of Tim's arm.

Tim instantly sensed his fear. "What's wrong" he said peering into the dark shadows, "did the mummy move, did she try to pick up her bones?

"No, you, silly sod, didn't you see the shadow that floated past the statue?" he whispered softly, as he glanced nervously around the dark recess near the statue.

Tim shook his head and moved closer to David.

"Something is watching us" David said apprehensively, as his eyes scanned the dark areas surrounding them, and felt a tingling sensation of fear run down his spine.

"Maybe," Tim replied, equally as tense and nervous, as he glanced anxiously about them. He they could only see the area where the light was shining otherwise everything was lost in the inky blackness of the chamber.

"Maybe it's the ghost of one of the women. Perhaps it's her arm we pulled off and she might want the ring back."

"Bloody hell, Tim, don't even think that."

Tim was silent for a few moments before asking. "What do you think it was?"

I don't bloody know. Come on, we're going to have to do this together" David indicated towards the dismembered limbs lying on the floor.

"The sooner we do this then the sooner we can leave."

It took almost an hour for Tim and David to replace and reset the limbs in order to make it appear that they had never been disturbed. The ring finger however, had been a problem as the finger had fallen apart and the hand had separated from the arm as soon as they had tried removing the ring. But after a brief struggle, they managed to reaffix the hand and finger the best they could. David then took the ring from Tim and slipped it into his pocket.

"I think we should come back after I've cleaned the ring and found out what these inscriptions mean."

"I agree, there's more to this than meets the eye. Anyway, we've got what we wanted so let's get out of here."

Giving a final glance about the chamber, Tim picked up the lamp and left locking the door securely behind them.

Chapter 34

CONTACTING THE POLICE

Tim contacted the police with regard to his findings in the chamber and told the police woman on the exchange, that it was a rather unusual and pretty grim situation.

He also informed her that there was no electricity in the chamber and as it was extremely dark in there, they would be needing extra strong lighting as the mummified bodies they had found were over a hundred years old. There were also many concealed alcoves and corners in which to search that he and David had missed.

"Mummies?" she asked in surprise.

"Yes, mummies," he replied starkly.

"Shouldn't you be calling the museum of archaeology?" she asked in a facetious tone.

Tim was in no mood to be wasting his time with the switchboard operator and was about to lose his temper. "Just do your job and put me through to someone in charge there;" He yelled.

"There isn't anyone available at the moment," she announced curtly.

By now Tim was fuming, "Listen to me," he shouted, then stopped what he was about say when David unexpectedly intervened and took the phone from his hand.

"Hello, who am I speaking to?" he asked calmly.

There was a silent hesitation for a few moments from the other end of the line.

"I am the Reverend David Hartley could you please tell me to who am I speaking?"

"Police Constable Jones," came the edgy reply.

"Alright, Police Constable Jones, we have a slight problem here at Church Cottage and we are asking for the police to investigate human remains that have been found in an underground chamber. The chamber has recently been discovered and there are three bodies chained to the walls."

David heard an audible gasp come down the line. "Now do you have anyone there in authority that I could speak to?"

"Hold the line and I will put you through to the Chief Constable."

David heard a click then silence before a deep voice boomed down the line.

"Chief Inspector Leonard Davies here, how can I be of assistance.?"

David began to explain the situation but didn't tell the Inspector everything. He did.

However, make it clear that they would be needing powerful lights with long lengths of cord as there was no electricity in the chamber. Also that there were three doors that were kept locked and there was a short, low passage they must go through before entering the chamber.

"You will find" he told the Inspector, "that there are power sockets inside the first crypt that Mr Bowman has installed. I will explain about the chamber when you arrive."

David ended the phone call before the Inspector began asking more questions.

Chapter 35

POLICE INVESTIGATION

"Before we start," Tim began, as he unlocked the first door allowing himself and David to lead the four police officers and Chief into the first crypt.

"The marks on the stone are blood stains from the vicar's victims, and are impossible to remove. They date back to the early 1900's, and the door you can see opposite where we are standing, is where we are going."

Tim didn't miss the look of apprehension that passed between the four officers.

"You can set the lights up in here." Tim pointed towards a set of light sockets near the door opposite. In the meantime, the chief inspector began asking questions about what had been discovered in the chamber.

"I can't put it into words what we found in there," David informed the Inspector.

"You will see for yourself when you get inside, and I can promise you it isn't nice."

The Inspector gave a grumpy acknowledgment and turned his attention back to his two officers who were assembling the lighting and adjusting the cables. They switched on the powerful lamps and immediately a brilliant glow filled the area.

"Alright you two, pick up the lamps and follow us," the inspector barked.

The men acknowledged they were ready to move they each and picked up the heavy lamps and waited until Tim had unlocked the second door, then with David leading the way, they moved steadily forward onto the stone steps leading down to the mysterious chamber. Tim unlocked the third and final door then turned to warn the officers that what they were about to see was not what they were accustomed to seeing. He opened the door, and stepped inside then stood back allowing the police officers to enter the chamber.

For a few seconds, every person was stunned into silence when the brilliant glow from the lamps lit up the entire chamber The shocking sight however was too much for two of the officers who couldn't deal with the horrendous vision in front of them. They looked at one another and raced away from the confines of their deadly surroundings, while the other two officers backed away to the open door not wanting to stay amongst the grotesque corpses.

The men had heard about the cursed haunted cottages and they glanced at one another apprehensively, undecided about whether to leave or to stay. Until the Inspectors voice boomed out telling them to pull themselves together and do the job they were there to do.

"What are we supposed to do? We can't do anything here, look at them?" exclaimed one of the officer's waving his arms in the air.

To Tim and David however, the three mummified corpses looked even worse than when they had first seen them, and the huge statue of the Knight's Templar warrior appeared even more lifelike and ferocious. His appearance was so credible that he looked as though he was about to step out of the wall and slaughter every last one of them. They also felt a sense of nausea when looking at the mummified corpses, and wondered how the devil they had managed to take the ring from one of the skeletal fingers.

The Chief Inspector and the two remaining officers were stunned and didn't know what to do, as they stared in horror at the three mummified skeletal corpses shackled to the throne like seats. The terrifying stare from sightless, stone eyes of the gigantic statue of the Templar warrior rendered them immobile, until the Inspector's voice boomed instructions to the them.

"Jackson, get onto forensics, Wright, you go upstairs with Jackson and don't let anyone down here, Father Hartley, Mr Bowman, would you mind leaving the chamber with me?

There is a slight possibility that no matter how small it is, any small iota of evidence that may still remain,could be destroyed by us fumbling about in here.

Chapter 36

FORENSIC INVESTIGATION

To the relief of everyone, the arrival of the forensic team who took over the investigation, informed everyone that they must not enter the chamber until they had completed a total examination of the crime scene.

"They will be lucky if they find anything," Tim whispered to David. "Just a moment," he called to the leading investigator. "You will be needing these," and he held out the keys.

Jane Holland, the forensic pathologist, took the proffered keys from his hand.

"Thanks."

"Don't touch anything else while you're down there. In fact I will come and make sure you don't."

Jane stopped and glared at Tim. "I would advise you to stay where you are."

"Like hell I will. This is my home and I will do as I like," he said angry at being ordered about in his own home, especially by a stranger.

"Tim" David placed a restraining hand on Tim's arm, "do as she says."

"They won't find anything in there," Tim grumbled softly, "the floor was cleaner than my front room."

"I couldn't agree with you more." David said. "Let's have a drink while we're waiting.

"What do you want? Tea? Coffee? Scotch?"

"Scotch, a large one."

"I know I shouldn't, but I will join you."

David poured them both a drink and sat down beside Tim.

Meanwhile, the Inspector and the two officers were only too pleased to get away from gruesome sight, and left the forensic team to examine and video the mummies, the statue, the sarcophagus, and the rest of the area before the mummified remains were removed and taken to the lab. There an examination would be carried out and hopefully, they would find evidence to determine the cause of death.

It was highly improbable though that anything could be found to identify the cause of the women's termination. There was a small glimmer of hope however, when back at the lab, Jane noticed that minute strands of all three women's hair was red. In her extensive experience it meant only one thing; the women had been poisoned. Whoever had carried out the procedure had done it in the manner of a ritual.

The entrails and the hearts had been placed in separate jars with the chest and stomach cavity carefully and meticulously stitched up. The jars were now on a shelf in her lab and Jane was hopeful that samples could be rescued from them.

Samples from the tufts of hair remaining on the skulls might also indicate what type of poison had been used.

She decided however, that the woman's deaths seemed rather unusual as they all appeared to have died and been incarcerated at the same time.

It was highly unlikely that all three women would have died a natural death at the same time. Also clearly visible on the video that Jane, could see, was that they had been seated and chained on a throne that had an inverted cross over their heads; they had been deliberately seated facing the marble sarcophagus opposite them.

The question was, WHY?

As the bodies had lain there undisturbed for a vast number of years, the police decided that there would be no hope of discovering who they were.

Whereby after the forensic people and the police had gathered up their equipment and left, Tim locked the chamber and returned upstairs with David to discuss what they should do next.

Chapter 37

TIM AND DAVID

The first thing that Tim did was to rent a series of arc lights similar to those the police had used in the chamber. Then he and David were able to examine the six feet high frescoes of various saints on the walls that they had missed previously.

Also the inscription on the plaque placed above the white marble sarcophagus.

"David, you should see this." Tim could hardly conceal his excitement when reading, Here lies the body of my scheming unfaithful wife, the whore Lady Catherine Von Platt.

"David." He called impatiently.

"Never mind that, Tim! Take a Look at this." David called from where he was examining A carved pouch on the statue.

Slightly disgruntled, Tim jumped down from the sarcophagus and went to David.

"Look here, what do you think this is?" David asked pointing to the warrior's pouch hung by his side. "It looks like runic symbols but I can't decipher them.

"I don't know," Tim mumbled, "maybe It's just something for decoration on his outfit. "Or it could be some form of protection that someone has carved there."

"Carving or not don't you think it is time that we had something to eat?" Tim stated, hearing his stomach begin to rumble.

"We've been down here for about four hours, come on there's cold meat in the fridge and hard boiled eggs."

Tim locked the door after them and they returned to the kitchen where he took the food from the fridge.

"What do you want tea, coffee or beer? He asked.

"Seeing as I'm staying over I wouldn't mind a beer" David replied.

"David?"

"What"

"Did you sense anything when the police were here?"

"Yes I did" David replied hesitantly, "And I think the Inspector did too, I did notice that he was jumpy and appeared to be watching something, but what I don't know.

"I also felt as if a great burden had been lifted when they removed those corpses from the crypt, but I did sense that something vindictive wanted us all out of there" he added.

"can't explain the weird sensation I was experiencing, but I can say for certain that it was evil."

Chapter 38

RITUAL ITEMS

Following a long discussion about what they should do next, Tim and David returned to the chamber where David prepared to carry out a blessing with help from Tim.

Before they had got started, Tim, who was examining one of the Frescoes of a saint on the wall, noticed a slight indentation on the saint's elaborately designed robe.

"David, can you come over here for a minute and take a look at this?"

David, who had been preoccupied with another painting moved over to Tim's side to see what he had found.

"Do you recognise this saint? and what does he represent?" Tim asked.

David stood shaking his head, he was as baffled as Tim.

"I've no idea who any of them are. In fact, neither does the bishop. I took photos of them earlier on my phone and sent them to him, he is just as puzzled as we are. He is checking up on them and will get back to me as soon as he has any further information.

"Can you see that red piece where his robe folds over the green?" Tim motioned towards a particular area of the saint's robe. "If you look closely you will see that it is more pronounced than the rest?"

For a few moments David studied the area where Tim was indicating.

"Yes, I can see it now that you've pointed it out. What do you think it is?"

"I don't know." Tim replied, fingering the artwork, then gave an exclamation of surprise when he felt it move.

"Oh shit, I hope I haven't damaged anything," he groaned, quickly pulling his hand away.

"I don't think so," David replied touching the fine art work, as he leant closer and put his hand on the section of the pleated area where Tim had felt the movement.

"You could be right," he concurred when feeling a slight quiver beneath his fingers.

Something did move," he said excitedly," I actually felt it."

Using extreme care so as not to damage the ancient artifact, David gently pressed against the raised, painted fold, and instantly felt a slight vibration run through his fingers, followed by a low rumbling sound.

They watched in awe as the shield alongside the legs of the Knights Templar swung to one side revealing a dense black hole.

"Oh my God," David exclaimed, crossing himself. "What on earth have we found?"

Tim could hardly conceal his excitement and leant towards the opening hoping to see what was inside.

"Wait!" David shouted. "Don't touch anything, it could be a trap."

Tim leapt back in alarm.

"It's dark in there, but it appears to be almost big enough for a man to crawl into,"

David said staring into the dark alcove.

"Hang on a minute while I use the light on my phone to see what's inside." David took his mobile from his pocket and shone the light into the recess.

"My God. Holy mother of Jesus," he muttered falling back onto the floor ashen faced.

"David, are you alright? Tim asked frantic to know what had caused his friend to react so badly that he had blasphemed.

"Take a look for yourself," David stammered, as he handed Tim his phone.

Tim knelt beside David and took the phone from his shaking hands then pressed the light button to see what was inside the alcove.

"Bloody hell," he muttered, astounded by what he was seeing piled inside. He could just make out a number of articles that were partially visible with the material that had mostly rotted and disintegrated over the years still wrapped around them.

The disintegrated material was now partly revealing what appeared to be a number of discoloured skulls, an assortment of dried up yellow bones, daggers, chalice's, and tarnished silver candlestick holders along with many other items.

At first Tim couldn't believe what he was seeing and turned to David, who acknowledged that he had also seen the same and nodded.

"We've got to get that stuff out of there and take a closer look at it," Tim declared.

"Then we can examine it properly."

"No," David's voice was stern as he spoke. "We leave everything just as it is, it is obvious that those items were used to procure evil forces." David rose to his feet.

"Whoever sealed this tomb did the right thing, every article and person who was placed in here must have been evil."

"Come on David, that's the church talking, you know as well as I do that we have just made an historical discovery."

"No," David argued. "What we have found is for the use of pure evil and I don't want any part of it neither should you."

"But David," Tim gestured helplessly, "they could be the answer to everything that's happening here." "Just let me take a couple of things from the front and leave the others that are stacked further behind, those small boxes for instance." He pointed to three boxes at the front of the other items.

After thinking for a few moments David relented and let Tim remove the three small wooden containers, that on close examination were found to contain various dried herbs and incense.

"Now that you have seen what they contain, you can put them back where they belong and let's get out of here." David declared in a sombre tone.

"Are you certain?"

David was in no mood to argue with him. "Yes, I'm certain, now come on" he said sharply as he moved towards the door.

"I said, Now, and make sure that the access is shut," he snapped irritably when Tim continued to peer into the cavity.

Tim reluctantly got to his feet and dusted his clothes down then pushed the shield back into place, and grumbling to himself, he followed David to the door.

"We are going to regret this you know I think we should-----"

"Forget about it," David interrupted, "we are leaving." He pushed Tim out of the open door.

"Lock it," he ordered and give me the key. I don't want you interfering with anything you don't understand. After I have left, I'm going to call the Archbishop for advice before we go any further."

Chapter 39

THE MEETING

After a tormented night's sleep, David contacted Bishop Johnson who spoke to Brother Armstrong, a priest of high order, asking if he would be willing to join him in conducting an exorcism at the macabre death chamber and cottage. He explained the dangerous situation he would be placing himself in, he was also given the choice of whether or not to take on the hazardous mission.

Brother Armstrong didn't hesitate in making his decision, he understood the desperate situation that the recipients found themselves in. He had also experienced the ungodly phenomenon first hand when he had undertaken a similar task in a different area of North Yorkshire a number of years ago.

"If I could survive that then I am certain that I can help this poor suffering man," he said to himself as he agreed to carry out the task.

When Bishop Johnson contacted David he advised him not to do anything foolish like re-entering the crypt, and told him it would take a number of days to prepare himself. He also had to collect all of the necessary items that he would require for the cleansing. It would then take another day for him and his assistant to reach that specific area of North Yorkshire and to find the cottage. The complete time span would take six days at the most.

Tim was concerned for the clergy's safety as he recalled that within hours of the police leaving and the forensic team removing the mummified bodies from the cottage. two of the officers were drowned when the driver lost control of his car and it skidded into the fast flowing river. The forensic investigators, who were present at the scene, had been admitted to hospital with broken bones and serious sprains and fractures of their limbs.

From what Tim knew it was a positive fact, that any person coming into contact with anything concerning the dark arts, will suffer leg, ankle, arm, wrist and hand injuries. (*TRUE*)

Tim pushed his doubts to one side when the day arose for the clergy men's arrival, and found himself pacing anxiously from one room to another while trying to set aside the nervous tension that was swirling about him. It was the same with James and David who had arrived the previous day.

At around 10-am they watched as a dark grey four-wheel drive vehicle pulled into the drive of the cottage.

"They're here that's the car," David announced, when seeing the insignia on the badge that was propped beside the windscreen. In an instant, David rushed outside to greet the two occupants and stood beside the vehicle ready to help, as they popped open the back door of the car for him to remove their luggage containing the articles they would be needing for the exorcism.

"Let's hope they can be of some help," Tim murmured to James as the trio made their way towards the open door of the cottage and came inside.

It is a proven fact that anyone coming into contact with anyone practicing the dark arts will receive damage to their arms legs and neck.

Chapter 40

THE DISCUSSION

"Tim, James, this is Bishop Johnson and Brother Armstrong," David said, introducing the four men to one another. Tim was surprised when seeing that the Bishop and Brother Armstrong were dressed casually in jeans and sweaters. Both sported grey hair and were about five feet ten inches tall, and were of solid build.

The Bishop didn't waste any time in asking if he could visit the chamber and see the bizarre contents for himself. Then he would decide when, or' if' there would be any need for an exorcism. If so he wanted to put together a plan of action together to protect not only himself, but everyone who was to be involved.

Tim and James glanced at one another in surprise at the bishop's unconventional request.

"Would you like a drink or something to eat before you begin?" David asked hesitantly, not wanting to say the wrong thing. "Or perhaps a short rest after your long Journey?"

"No thank you," the Bishop replied smiling pleasantly as he spoke. "You should understand, that, when we are dealing with the occult, it is always preferable to work on an empty stomach, especially when we don't know what force of energy we are going to be dealing with. And we don't want to be needing the bathroom do we?"

Brother Armstrong agreed, although he was aware of a presence nearby that was studying them and listening to the plans they were making. The invisible entity was also scheming and it had already decided that it would take control of anyone who went near the secret chamber with its concealed, disturbing, deadly contents.

"What can we have to do to help with the exorcism?" James asked. He was filled with excitement at the prospect of becoming involved in the exorcism of a supernatural being for the first time.

"Yes, that's what I would like to know?" Tim added, "what can we do?"

"You can stay out of our way" the bishop added in a solemn tone.

"You can stay here in this room, Brother David will stay with you, as he understands how to protect you from any evil phenomenon that may occur or make itself known."

Tim could hardly believe what he was hearing. "Can't I at least stay and wait outside the chamber until you-------"

"No" the Bishop stated patiently, waving Tim's protests to one side.

"From now on I am responsible for your safety, therefore I do not want anything occurring that Brother Armstrong, Brother David or I cannot control. You must give me your word that you will stay in this room with Brother David and under no circumstances must you leave his side, he will bequeath all the protection that you will be needing. Brother Armstrong is strong enough to face any unforeseen dangers that could lay ahead. Not only a is he a priest but he is also a psychic and will warn me of any danger that could be lurking nearby."

"Now if you will excuse me, Brother Armstrong and I must prepare for what we were brought here to do."

The Bishop gave a dismissive wave of his hand. "I believe that Brother Johnson and I should be leaving to take a look at the chamber."

Chapter 41

THE CHAMBER OF HORRORS

As the two clergy men rose to their feet David handed the Bishop the keys to each door leading to the chamber.

"Please be careful," he warned, "there are many hidden dangers that cannot be seen down there."

"God is with us my son you protect these men." the Bishop said throwing a noncomital glance towards Tim and James as he placed a comforting arm on David's shoulder. The Bishop then turned and left followed by Brother Armstrong They had both been briefed on how to get to the chamber and how to open the hidden alcove.

In silence, the Bishop and Brother Armstrong made their way along the hallway then stopped to open the basement door and proceeded down the stairs into the games room. They passed through into the gymnasium. Where the Bishop stopped to unlock the door allowing them to enter the first crypt. He hesitated for a few moments after noticing the discoloured blood stains on the stone slabs as they walked by.

Thankfully, the power point was body height and near to the door leading down to the second chamber. Following Tim's instructions the Bishop told Johnson to plug in and switch on the arc light. He then proceeded to unlock the door and opened it.

Immediately, the eerie blackness was lit by a brilliant glow of white light that illuminated a low stone passage.

For a moment, Brother Armstrong hesitated, feeling a sense of unease, but brushed it to one side presuming that it could have been just his nerves acting up by being in unknown territory. His hesitation however, had not gone unnoticed by the Bishop who asked if he was alright, and if he felt it safe to carry on.

Armstrong nodded, acknowledging that everything was fine, but his gut was churning at the thought of what lay ahead. He picked up the heavy lamp and made his way through the low arched doorway and down the steps into the narrow passage.

Then he stopped when he approached the door of the gruesome death chamber.

"If you don't mind me saying you're Grace, I don't like the feel of this."

Armstrong said in a solemn tone, shaking his head.

The Bishop acknowledged what Armstrong was saying and nodded, he then crossed himself and while saying a prayer of protection for them both, he stepped forward and unlocked and allowed the door to swing wide open.

They were in for an unprecedented shock when they entered the chamber and were met by the ferocious stare of the Knights Templar statue standing directly in front of them.

"Merciful heaven may God protect us," the Bishop muttered as he stared at the incredible structure.

Armstrong was equally shocked but quickly regained his composure.

"This must have been where the three mummies were seated," he said indicating the now empty thrones and the shackles left in the walls.

"And, your Grace, isn't this where the inverted crosses were placed above each mummy that was chained to the thrones?" Armstrong asked, pointing to the outline were the crosses had been placed.

"Yes," the Bishop agreed, "and from the photographs that I have here, they were facing the sarcophagus opposite.

"Good grief," he murmured, when reading the inscription that Tim had brushed clean enabling him to see what was written.

"Why on God's earth should someone have wanted to write those disparaging words above the woman's sarcophagus?" The Bishop stood, shaking his head.

"It makes me wonder if any of those three women, and the woman in the sarcophagus, had been involved in some form of ritual magic, or if not, then was it the person who had placed them there."

"It most likely was," Armstrong added thoughtfully.

"Perhaps the women were innocent of any wrong-doing and the person who killed them and placed them in here, was involved in the evil side of the occult. They were most likely a sacrifice to whatever he, or she, believed in."

"You could be right" the Bishop, agreed, "and whoever discovered the bodies before the tomb was sealed, didn't want any of the evil in there to escape and contaminate more innocent souls."

For a short while the Bishop stood and pondered thoughtfully before commenting further. "It is a small possibility that whoever found those pour souls wanted to protect them and they could have recited prayers over their dead bodies, in an effort to drive out the evil that had been carried out around them, before sealing the chamber."

He turned his attention towards the unrecognisable faces of the unidentified Saints, saying that they should examine them more closely.

"I cannot recognise any of these saints, that's if they are saints," The Bishop commented as he steadily made his way past each one, halting only momentarily to scrutinise each painting as he peered intently at them. "I'm afraid they don't belong to any order that I have ever seen" he said thoughtfully.

"Brother Armstrong, can you direct the light over here?" he called to his colleague.

"I want to see what is in the alcove when we open it."

Armstrong angled the arc light so that it shone directly onto the warrior's shield in front of the statue.

"Thank you, that is perfect," the Bishop said, "it will enable us to see what is inside the camouflaged recess once we get it open."

Brother Armstrong moved over to the painting of the saint and felt along the pleated area of the painting until he felt the raised area that Tim had spoken of, then pressed against the fold of its robe. Immediately, the shield swung away from the Templar revealing the hidden relics of the secret alcove.

"Dear God," they both exclaimed, crossing themselves while uttering a quiet prayer, as the glowing light revealed the gruesome sight of unusual hidden relics from the past.

After overcoming the shock of what they had stumbled upon, Brother Armstrong began removing some of the articles from the alcove.

Satin and velvet altar cloths that were embroidered with pure silk were neatly folded in a plain hessian material that had protected them from the ravages of time.

There were golden goblets studded with precious stones; hand cut glass decorative decanters; tall black candles carved with magic symbols that would only have been used when conducting a black mass service to contact evil spirits, gem-studded daggers, wands, and other items, along with a number of dismembered mummified animal remains, plus a number of human skulls and human bones.

Adding to the unexpected shock of what the alcove revealed was the fact that all of the relics appeared to be in perfect condition.

The one that shocked them the most was the inverted cross of Christ.

It was then they fully realised that they had stumbled across something more deadly and sinister than they had ever expected to find, a Satanic chamber.

The Bishop was the first to recover from the shock.

" Don't touch anything more," he said softly. Put it all back" he ordered in a soft monotone.

Brother Armstrong glowered at him with a strange look on his face. Immediately, the Bishop realised that something was amiss.

"I said put it back now, this place is cursed, I recognise the strange symbols on the walls, they are a runic curse. We have to get away from here immediately."

Still Brother Armstrong hesitated, unsure of what to do as he clutched one of the golden relics in his hands.

"I have just told you to put it all back," the Bishop snapped, snatching the chalice from Armstrong and casting it back into the recess.

"Now we must return and tell Mr Bowman of our findings."

Chapter 42

JAMES SISTER MORTICIA

Tim and James were fuming over being left out of the investigating the burial chamber with the clergy men. They agreed that after what had happened to Julia, the Bishop was right in regard to everyone's safety, and they had sent the children away.

In the meantime, while they were sat waiting for the Bishop to report his findings, out of the blue James announced a staggering statement.

"Tim," James paused for a moment as if searching for the right way to put forward what he wanted to say to his friend.

"Yes," Tim replied. From the look on Jame's face it was obvious that something was troubling him.

"If anything should happen to me, I don't want my sister or any of her family to attend my funeral."

Tim's jaw dropped. "What?" his tone was one of shock and disbelief.

"You're not ill, are you? If you are why didn't you say something before.?"

"No," James replied in a voice filled with adversity."

"It's nothing like that."

"Then what is it?" He waited patiently for James to say what was troubling him.

"It's about my sister," he began.

"Oh no, not her," Tim groaned, and felt a warning light go on. He was aware that through no fault of his own, James and Portia hadn't spoken for many years.

He did however, believe that from her erratic behaviour over the years she must have some sort of a mental problem. "Go on tell me what's bothering you?" he cajoled.

"It's about my brother in law George"

"What has he done now?"

"He's dead."

"What? When? How?" Tim was aghast, he couldn't stop the flow of questions recalling that the three of them used to get together once a month to go on fishing trips.

Before Portia had put a stop to it, she had demanded that he drop all of his old friends, leaving him lonely and friendless like herself.

"Cancer," James' voice interrupted Tim's thoughts. "It appears that he'd been ill for a long time but not one member of his family had the decency to tell me. It was a neighbour who informed me of his death. Anyway it wasn't until I arrived at the church to attend the funeral and introduced myself, that the invited guests realised that Portia had a brother. She had denied any existence of me they believed that she was an only child.

"The bitch" Tim cursed when feeling himself filling with rage at what Portia had done to her brother.

"After the funeral one of the men took me to one side and told me that nobody liked her and it was only out of respect for George that they had attended the funeral."

"Bloody hell, and you've been keeping it bottled up all this time. Why the hell didn't you say something before now? I thought we were friend's" Tim snapped angrily.

James sat shaking his head, he could not find an excuse for his sister's diabolical behaviour over the years.

"Before I die, I want you to let everyone know what a cruel controlling sadist bitch my sister really is.

"James nothing is going to happen you" Tim expressed loudly.

"Please Tim, hear me out, what I am about to say isn't going to be easy" James expressed in a voice filled with emotion.

Tim waited to hear what James had to add further, he began thinking of how Portia had suddenly cut herself off from James after their mother's death.

She hadn't even informed him when their father was admitted to hospital. If it hadn't been for his late brother-in-law George's unexpected arrival at his home, James would never have known that their father was ill.

George had begged James not to let Portia know that he had been to his house, as, like the rest of her family, he was scared to death of her.

James thanked him, then after George left, James had raced to the hospital. When he arrived he was stunned when his father made it quite clear that he was not welcome and that he should leave.

What his father said next was akin to having a knife driven into his stomach and slowly turned, when in a malicious tone, he told James, with a sardonic grin on his face, that he wasn't his real father and didn't know who was.

James had felt gutted, until two weeks later the final bombshell was dropped; when a neighbour rang to offer her condolences after she had seen his father's obituary in the local newspaper.

Portia nor any member of her family had the decency to inform him of his father's death. James had been devastated by both his sister's and fathers callous actions and words.

Chapter 43

THE DISCUSSION

Upon the return of the two clergymen, it was obvious from their behaviour and demeanour, that what they had seen in the chamber had deeply disturbed them both.

At first Tim was concerned for the pair, but the Bishop pushed his worries to one side by saying not to worry and that everything would be alright. In the meantime, James had managed to regain his self-control and had gone into the kitchen to prepare tea and sandwiches, then brought them through for the two clergymen.

Much to the Bishop and Brother Armstrong's disapproval however, Tim had poured himself and James a large tumbler filled with whisky and had drunk half the contents in minutes before returning for a refill.

After they had finished eating the Bishop began revealing what they had found in the chamber, and that he needed to speak with them both before conducting the exorcism.

He asked Tim, if he could explain in detail what he and the others had experienced at the cottage and especially what had occurred when they first opened the chamber.

Tim and James explained in detail what they had discovered and what they had experienced. They also believed that Julia's death was linked to the moment they they opened the door and entered the chamber.

"I wish Jessica had never brought the blasted plans and photographs," Tim moaned in anguish as he flopped down onto the sofa and hid his face in his hands.

"It's all my fault she's dead," he sobbed.

Bishop Johnson and Brother Armstrong gave one another a quizzical glance before asking. "What photographs and plans are you talking about?"

"I'll show you," said Tim.

James told Tim to stay where he was while he got to his feet and hurried over to the desk and took out the printed copies of the old church before it was burnt down and after. He then handed the Bishop a magnifying glass to enable him to closely examine the photographs of the burnt out church when it was being turned into cottages. He also showed him the photos depicting the weird oddities in the woods that were amongst the people watching while the cottages were being built.

The clergymen couldn't help but gasp from time to time as they sifted through the drawings and photos noticing the mutilated corpses hanging amongst the shrubbery and trees.

"It appears that many bad things have occurred here," the Bishop said, rubbing his brow thoughtfully. He began asking questions regarding the recent hauntings both inside and out of the cottage, and about the chamber where the mummified bodies had been discovered.

But as soon as Tim began explaining their findings, and the strange phenomena that were occurring, the door of the lounge unexpectedly flung itself wide open causing Tim to leap up in alarm.

"Please. sit down," Brother Armstrong spoke in a calm soothing tone.

"There is no reason for you to be alarmed, the presence will not harm you."

An uneasy glance passed between Tim and James, then towards David, who appeared to be unruffled by what was happening.

"Brother Armstrong is right, please accept what he has told you and resume your Seats," David announced in a solemn tone.

Tim was about to argue when he looked over at James, who passed him a knowing look, motioning with his eyes for Tim to sit down.

Tim was concerned by David's manner and wondered if something had occurred about which that he and James were unaware while they were in the chamber. In spite of what they were discussing Tim kept an observant eye on David, watching for any irregularities in his behaviour. He was also aware that both the Bishop and Armstrong were watching David as he appeared to be anxious and nervy about what they were discussing.

"Brother David" the sharp note in the Bishop's voice cut through the strange silence that had suddenly enveloped the room.

David didn't reply.

"David" James spoke sharply, "David, snap out of it" he commanded.

"What? oh sorry, Bishop Johnson, what were you saying?" David suddenly felt his face redden with embarrassment. He shook his head trying to clear away the confused thoughts that had unexpectedly began to filter through his mind.

In his mind's eye, all David could see was the figure of a tall, muscular man, who was stamping his feet like a mad bull, and cursing as he raged in a blind fury about the chamber.

Chapter 44

THE MEDIA

The abrupt sound of the telephone ringing broke the silence that had fallen on each person seated in the room, causing them to flinch, and stare anxiously at one another.

"It can't be business," Tim muttered, getting to his feet', or whoever it was would have called on my mobile and left a message.

Annoyed by the interruption, Tim excused himself and went to answer the phone then slammed the receiver down in anger upon hearing someone from the media asking for an interview regarding the three mummified corpses found at his home.

"How the devil have they found out so quickly?" he ranted, turning accusingly to face James who gave an involuntary gesture with his hands.

Then as he was about to return to his seat, Tim noticed someone peering at him through the window.

"What the hell," he cursed hurrying over to the window and drawing the curtains but not before he noticed a large group of people and TV cameras, plus various members of the media who had converged outside the cottage gate and were now unlawfully encroaching onto his property.

James had raced over to the landline phone and unplugged it just as his and Tim's mobile phones began ringing.

"Oh shit," James mumbled as he saw an unrecognised number on the screen and immediately switched off his phone and put it on mute. Tim thinking it was business, answered his mobile, and was shocked when it was a member of the television company parked outside of his property asking for an interview. They asked if Tim would allow them to film inside the crypt where the mummified bodies had been discovered.

For a moment Tim was too shocked to reply until James, who was furious by the invasion of their privacy, snatched the mobile from Tim's hands and switched it off.

Then raced to the front of the cottage and locked the door while Tim hurried to lock the back door and began drawing the curtains in every room, but not before noticing that in the woodland behind them, was the swaying corpse of the evil vicar who had slaughtered his entire family.

Chapter 45

PANIC

"Ring the police, get them out of here," David shouted hysterically. They should be looking at what's behind them in the woods, not trying to find out what's happening in here.

Brother Armstrong could clearly see that David was greatly distressed and moved over to the window and peered outside.

"Oh my God, heaven protect us" he gasped. He crossed himself when he saw the partially decayed corpse of the long dead vicar standing, minus his head, just a few yards behind the media, whose attention was focused on the cottage.

Suddenly, a loud scream filled the air and everyone outside, turned then dropped silent when seeing the repugnant apparition standing behind them.

The sounds of shrieking hysteria and the wailing of approaching police cars did little to ease the nerves of the people, both inside and outside of the cottage. When cameras, microphones and other electrical paraphernalia were dropped to the ground as the reporters scrambled to escape from the grotesque creature standing amongst them as chaos exploded all around.

Chapter 46

THE POLICE

"You must expect the press to be inquisitive after something like this has occurred," the Bishop said with a quivering voice after peering through the window.

Where he could see the hysterical men and women scrambling over one another to reach the safety of their vehicles. While others were trying desperately to film the gruesome spectre behind them, and the other hideous abominations that were hanging from the trees in the forest.

The Bishop was interrupted in what he was saying when two bearded police officers drew up in a squad car and got out. After pushing their way through the panicking crowd of reporters and sightseers they knocked at the door of the cottage.

"Oh God, not now," James moaned, as Tim went over to the door to let them in.

"I'm Sergeant Barnes and this is Sergeant Jones," Barnes said, at the same time as they removed their caps and followed Tim along the hallway into the lounge.

"Oh, I see you have company," Barnes nodded an apology when observing the Bishop and Brother Armstrong seated in the front room.

"I'm sorry to intrude, but this won't take long. Could we have a word in private, sir?" he asked Tim as all eyes turned towards him.

"It's alright officer, whatever you have to say can be said in front of everyone here,"

Tim indicated for the two officers to be seated, and explained to them why the light was switched on and why they'd had to close the drapes.

"I understand sir." Barnes gave a nervous cough, as he was unused to being in the company of members of the clergy.

"We came after someone made a complaint from this address, that vehicles were blocking the lane and trespassers were on your property," he announced more sharply than meant to.

"But after seeing first-hand what is happening outside, well, I can say in all honesty, it gave me and the lads quite a shock."

He was just about to add more, when a loud thud echoed from the ground below.

"Is anyone down there?" The sergeant asked leaping to his feet, while at the same time giving Tim a suspicious look.

"It isn't a game sir. Now if you are hiding someone who…….."

Barnes broke off what he was about to say when a piercing scream came from below and echoed all around the cottage.

"What the devil" he snapped. "Jones take two men with you and find out what's going on in the cellar."

Tim was about to say something, but it was too late, Jones was already calling outside for the two officers who had been taking statements to assist him in searching the rooms below. Amid the confusion David had placed a restraining hand on Tim's arm and silently shook his head, gesturing for him to shut up and sit down.

James, however, got up and left the lounge to guide the officers to the door leading to the rooms below and switched on the light, then hastily returned to re-join the others.

"Right then who's opening the door?" Officer Brill who was in charge asked the two men who were stood waiting uneasily for someone to make the first move.

"For goodness sake" he muttered, pushing past them and opening the door.

"Is the force requiting a bunch of fucking wimps or what?"

With the two men, he stepped inside onto the wide stone slab leading down the steps into the basement. But as soon as they were inside they stopped and stared in stunned amazement, as everything suddenly changed.

Instead of the games room they saw a vast open area and the shimmering apparitions of a group of ghostly women from a past era scrubbing their weekly wash.

They heard the sound of running water, the mangle being turned and the squeak of a drying rack on which the washing was hung to dry as it was hoisted up towards the ceiling. There were also six women toiling with heavy shovels as they scraped along the floor gathering coal to stoke the slate boilers to keep the water hot.

Worse was yet to come, when an old farmer appeared herding a group of sheep into the stone flagged cellar, where he systematically began cutting their throats and disembowelling them.

"Fucking hell one of the officers groaned feeling his stomach heave."

"I agree," Officer Brill whispered hoarsely, unable to cast his eyes away from the macabre sight.

"What do we do now?" Simpson's voice quivered as he spoke.

"We get the hell out of here," Brill responded, glancing tentatively around them. "The sooner the better."

"Look," Officer Brill said pointing to the figures. Everyone watched as the ungodly apparitions steadily faded away.

"Holy Moses," Brill whispered, more to himself than the others. "I wouldn't have believed it if I hadn't seen it for myself."

Simpson didn't wait to see any more, but raced out of the basement and cottage to the waiting police car. He jumped inside, locked the doors and sat cowering as he glanced fearfully around outside.

"Come on we're getting out of here," Barnes exclaimed, then glanced over at Brill who was stood shaking and unmoving and staring down into the now empty games room.

"Oh no!," the sergeant moaned, it was obvious that Brill was in shock.

"Come on your safe with me, he said taking hold of the trembling man's arm and leading him out of the basement. Once they were clear Baxter slammed the door shut and led Brill along the hallway and into the lounge, where a number of anxious faces turned towards them.

"We have just witnessed something unusual down below," Baxter's voice trembled he spoke. "It has greatly distressed two of my men, one of them ran outside and this officer was incapacitated with fear and he is in shock. Would it be alright if he sat down for a few moments to recover?" he asked shakily.

"Of course," Tim took hold of the officer's arm and led him to the chair to sit him down.

"You look as if you need to sit down as well." He told Baxter offering him a seat.

"I'll get them both a drink," James offered, and hurried over to the cabinet to pour a dram of whiskey for both men.

"You will never believe what we saw down there, by the way did anyone see where officer Simpson went?" Baxter asked, staring round at the anxious inquiring faces.

"We heard someone dash down the corridor and go outside" the Bishop replied.

"Tell me did you all see the same thing?" he asked in a monotone voice.

"Yes," Baxter replied. "But what we saw is almost unbelievable," Baxter had to place the tumbler onto the table, as he was beginning to feel the effect of the ghastly encounter and could hardly stop shaking.

"We're waiting," Tim snapped, impatient to find out what had caused the men to become so distressed.

Baxter's voice trembled as he spoke. "As soon as we stepped into the games room it changed into a cellar where we saw a group of peasant women scrubbing clothes, and they were talking to one another."

"How many were there?" the Bishop asked, rising from his seat to stand beside Baxter.

"At a rough guess about fifteen to twenty of them, aged between twenty and forty.

It's hard to say as they aged fast in those days didn't they, the poor sods. There was also a number of youngsters running around and little ones laid in clothes baskets.

"Was there anything else? Any men, young or old? Anything different about the people?"

"No, but you are going to find this hard to believe; after the women disappeared we all saw an old farmer bring in some sheep and slaughter them. Where the hell he came from I don't rightly know."

"That would have been Old Jake" Tim whispered nervously, scanning the room around him. "I should have known that old bugger would still be about"

"What else did you see? Did you venture any further than the steps?" the Bishop asked.

"No sir, as I told you, there were only washer women and children down there."

"Here, drink this," James came to Baxter's side and handed him another glass of whiskey.

"I hope it helps you to feel better."

"Thanks" Baxter said as he took the offered drink, then almost dropped it when an unearthly scream echoed from below.

"Oh God, not again," he said in a voice trembling with fear, "I'm not going back down there."

Chapter 47

THE CALM

A cold, nerve-wracking sense of unease gathered around the six disquieted people gathered in the room. Only the Bishop, Brother Armstrong and David remained calm nobody else dared move.

"Stay where you are," the Bishop commanded.

"The entity is only trying to frighten us. If you remain calm and carry on as you normally do, speak of any interests that may have, but carry on as if you have not heard a thing, do you understand?"

James was the first to acknowledge the instruction and he immediately grasped the meaning of what the bishop was saying. Although he was feeling uneasy, James glanced at the worried faces of the men who had leapt to their feet the instant they had heard the horrific scream.

James however told them to remain calm and sit down to discuss the recent sports matches they had recently seen on television. To his relief Sergeant Baxter and Officer Brill who had now overcome their initial shock, understood what he was attempting to do and joined in.

This gave the Bishop the opportunity to concentrate on what was occurring in the cottage. He was acutely aware of the unsettling atmosphere that was slowly drifting into the room and settling all around them. But he didn't say anything to the men as they were already afraid and he didn't want to alarm them any further. Instead, he began uttering silent words of prayer as he moved slowly about the room giving protection to everyone in there.

David had noticed the unease and tension that was building and observed the dark shadow that was being pushed ahead of the Bishop as he circled everyone until reaching the open door, he went out into the hallway.

But as he did so David was gripped by a sense of alarm he didn't want the Bishop to be left alone with the entity. Inconspicuously he signalled for Brother Armstrong to follow him and watched anxiously as the Bishop approached the basement.

At the same time James had walked across the room to the open door hoping to see where the Brother Armstrong was going, but he quickly ground to a halt when something caught his eye in the wall mirror.

"Oh shit," he groaned perceiving the top half of a man's image reflecting in the glass standing behind himself and Tim. The man was a tall, muscular and handsome in a rugged way. A scar ran the entire length of his face from his forehead to his chin; his skin was tanned and weathered; his long dark brown hair was tied at the back of his head and he had piercing, pale blue grey eyes. He wore a black frock coat, a white shirt with a stiff white cravat and matching white cuffs.

At first,James was too surprised to say anything, then gathering his wits about himself he whirled around, but to his surprise he saw no one there. Upon returning his gaze to the mirror he saw the same man standing directly behind him.

For a few seconds, James held back the panic that was building inside of him, knowing that the Bishop and Armstrong had left the room, and David was stood in the hallway watching the Bishop and Armstrong as they descended into the basement.

He began frantically searching his mind for a reasonable explanation for of whom it could be, until a sudden unexpected thought occurred to him.

'No, it can't be! But his face is identical to the one on the statue in the crypt.

"Oh God," James felt sick to his stomach when realizing who the man could be. He didn't dare look away as the man appeared to be watching him, then after staring at one another for a few nerve-wracking moments, he disappeared.

James was too afraid to move as at any moment he was expecting the apparition to reappear. But when it didn't, James shifted his glance towards Tim's reflection in the mirror, who appeared to be totally unaware of what had been standing behind him.

The two remaining police officers had by now, made a hasty retreat and were on their way back to the station to report their findings. Leaving Tim, James and the clergy alone to deal with the mysterious entities and phenomena.

Chapter 48

RENTING THE COTTAGE

James was surprised to find Tim in a foul mood stamping about his office in frustration.

"Thank goodness the children aren't witnessing any of this," he snapped angrily.

"Now we've got silly buggers who call themselves, Paranormal Hunters writing and phoning to ask if they can come to investigate the property. Huh." he muttered, giving a disgruntled grunt.

"If they were to witness what we have then they'd wish they'd never asked."

"I agree with you there," James replied. "It's my opinion that they would make matters worse if they were to use Ouija boards and other paraphernalia."

"You would think that the police would stop the media and public from taking photos of the cottage and woods," Tim grumbled. "But no, they are too scared to come near the place."

"What the hell am I going to do? I've put all the money I had into the renovation of the cottage, I can't just pack up and leave now." Tim slumped down into the chair rubbing his head in frustration.

"The fucking place has killed Julia and broken my family life I can't take anymore."

To James' embarrassment Tim began sobbing and couldn't stop.

"There is another solution" James proffered hesitantly placing a hand on Tim's shoulder.

"Oh yes, and what's that?" Tim glared at him as he waited for James to offer a solution that would end all of his woes.

"Well, for a start," James began, then stopped when noticing the look of apprehension on Tim's face.

"This is only a suggestion." He held up his hand before Tim could say anything noticing an argumentative look cross his face.

"We could put an advertisement in the paper offering to rent the cottage to people who are deadly earnest, (excuse the pun) in investigating the paranormal. You could state that the rental must be for a month and the fee to be paid in advance, and charge a phenomenal price. That way you will start to recover some of your finances.

With the interest shown by the media regarding the hauntings and whatever was in the crypt at the time, as well as the clergy being involved. I believe you should reap a good profit from the income. You never know, someone might not be put off by the haunting and offer to purchase the cottage."

Tim stared at him in amazement. "Why didn't I think of that?" he said with a look of gratitude spreading across his face, and got up from the chair to clasp James' hand.

"You are a genius," he said patting his friend's shoulder. "I don't know what the hell I would do without you. Let's do it."

Chapter 49

WHERE ARE THEY

"What do you think is taking the Bishop and brother Armstrong so long?" Tim asked, casting a furtive glance towards James, as they stood impatiently waiting for a sign or a signal that everything was alright down below.

"I've no idea," James replied, with a puzzled frown on his face, "the last I saw of them they were going down into the chamber to prepare for the exorcism, and your pal Reverend David was at the basement door watching them go."

"I don't like this," Tim gestured towards the basement, "it's been nearly two hours since they left, surely we should have heard something from them by now?"

Tim went over to the open door and into the hall. "I'm not, happy about it either," he said, scanning the hallway in both directions.

"There's no sign of David either, so something must have happened, I can feel it, something's wrong." He threw a furtive glance at James.

"Do you think he could be with the Bishop?"

"It's possible," James replied, "but the Bishop did tell him to stay here with us."

They stood for a few moments wondering what to do until Tim made his decision.

"I'm going to take a look below to see if he is there, are you coming?"

James rolled his eyes and groaned, the last thing he wanted was to go back into the chamber. But he did however, feel a sense of responsibility towards the clergy as it had been a joint decision between Tim and himself for them to come and carry out the exorcism.

"I asked if you were coming," Tim snapped impatiently as he left the room.

James grunted a reply then stopped for a moment to pick up and pull on a warm sweater before following Tim along the hallway towards the basement door.

They gave a sigh of relief when finding David standing on the top step awaiting the Bishop's signal informing that everything was going according to plan.

"How's it going down there?" Tim asked peering as far as he could into the games room. From where he was standing at the top of the steps, even with the light burning brightly, he didn't have much of a vantage point in seeing very far.

"I haven't heard a sound," David responded passing a concerned glance towards the chamber and wringing his hands in frustration at being unable to join the Bishop.

"I am pleased that you're here though." He turned towards Tim." I do feel that I should go to the chamber to check that the Bishop and Brother Armstrong are alright.

"That's fine by us, but just be careful and let us know if you need any help." Tim replied.

A look of gratitude and relief spread across David's face, as he turned and quickly made his way down the steps and across the games room before disappearing from view.

Chapter 50

INSIDE THE CHAMBER

As David made his way across the first crypt towards the chamber he was surprised to see only darkness ahead. For a moment he hesitated when knowing that the area should have been well illuminated. Then he shuddered as there was a sudden drop in the temperature that began surrounding him and appeared to be emanating from the chamber.

'This isn't right,' he thought to himself, 'I know the crypt is well below ground level but it shouldn't be so cold in there." All of sudden David felt a sense of unease and anxiety run through him, when feeling that something was terribly amiss. He felt a cold trickle of fear run down his spine inducing him to stop for a few moments and pause before deciding that he wasn't about to enter the dark foreboding crypt alone, and that he needed someone with him to ensure his safety.

As he stood there shivering he was thankful that he was wearing a thick woolly sweater, jeans and heavy soled boots. Within moments however, his thoughts were interrupted when a series of loud bangs began echoing about him and he watched in dread as a frosty current of cold air swirled towards him.

In an instant David sensed that a tremendous danger was approaching and grabbed hold of the sturdy cross he wore around his neck "God protect me," he murmured softly and prayed as he watched the abnormal force approaching slowly towards him as it ominously flowed from the chamber.

Although terrified, David felt as though he shouldn't turn his back from wherever the weird phenomenon was emanating. Instead, he retreated backwards away from it until he felt the heels of his boots touch the lowest of the steps.

Keeping a watchful eye on the weird, unearthly substance he retreated slowly, edging his way up, one step at a time until he reached the top of the stairs.

He then hurried through the open doorway, slammed the door shut behind him and leant against it gasping for breath, grateful that he had made it out in one piece, and thanking the holy saints for his wellbeing.

Chapter 51

WHAT HAPPENED

To Tim and James' amazement, when David came staggering into the lounge they could hardly understand a word that he was trying to say.

"David, calm down," James said, taking hold of his arm and trying to get him to sit down, but David pushed his hands away.

"No, there's no time, you've got to come now," he said, breaking away from James' grip.

"There is no light in the chamber the electricity isn't working, it's gone off" David yelled as the hysteria rose in his voice.

"And the Bishop and Brother Armstrong are in there."

"What?" Tim almost chocked on his words feeling a surge of dread run through him.

"I said there is no light in the chamber, and something is wrong, the Bishop and Brother Armstrong are not answering when I call their names.

"Oh my God," Tim groaned, then threw James a look of caution before springing into action.

"I'll get one of my work lamps and we can use that"

"Where is it? I'll get it, James offered, hurrying to the door.

"It's in the shed outside," Tim called after him.

"Have you got a torch" David urged, "then I can get back down there and see what's happening."

"You are not going back on your own. You will wait for James to bring the lamp" Tim told him in no uncertain terms.

"You don't know what could be waiting to pounce, it could be dangerous.

Just then James returned with the lamp.

"Right everybody, let's go. Tim took the heavy industrial lamp from James and headed for the basement, then stopped at the door to issue a solemn warning.

"I don't have to warn you that this could be dangerous," he remarked harshly glancing from James to David.

"We know that" David replied, "but the Bishop-----"

"We're in this together," James butted in giving a gesture of defiance.

Cautiously they made their way down the steps across the cellar past the first crypt until they reached the doorway leading to the second chamber and saw that everything beyond was in total darkness.

"I don't like this, the electrics should be working," Tim said, reaching for the wall switch, then gave an exclamation of surprise. "Somebody has turned it off." They all stared at one another in disbelief.

"Why would someone do that" David murmured softly, "Unless."

Oh my God!" he shrieked, when Tim switched on the light to expose the motionless figures of Bishop Johnson and Brother Armstrong, kneeling, rooted to the spot with a look of stark terror on their faces.

They were staring directly ahead at the statue of the Knight Templar who appeared almost lifelike in the weird shadows that were cast in the creepy chamber.

"Bloody Hell," Tim uttered quietly, unable to take his eyes away from the gruesome spectacle in front of him.

"What the devil," James remarked moving towards the two men, but David grasped his arm to stop him from moving forward.

"Don't go near them," David whispered, "they are already dead."

"What do you mean they are dead" James hissed as he tried to break away from David's firm grip.

"Can't you see you fool that they have been frightened to death look at their faces."

For a moment James stopped fighting with David, and stared at the two rigid figures before the realisation sank in that they were no longer living.

"What on earth could have happened?" he uttered and leant on David for support.

"Only ungodly forces could have carried out such a sacrilege as this" David said quietly, distressed by the sight of what was in front of him.

Chapter 52

JAMES

"You mean? Oh no! No," James shouted as the shock and sudden realisation of the situation became too much for him to bear. Without warning, he lashed out at David and broke free from his protective hold, as he ran screaming from the crypt, through the two rooms and up the stairs into the hall.

He grabbed his car keys from the hall table and dashed outside, jumped into his car, and terror-stricken, he drove away at breakneck speed. At that moment all James could think of was getting away from the evil presence in the cottage that had killed the two clergymen. He was not thinking of the treacherous weather conditions that he was now driving through.

Within ten minutes of him driving away, James had to slam his foot down hard on the brake pedal to bring his vehicle to a skidding halt, when a woman appeared directly ahead of him out of the blanket of falling snow.

Bracing himself for the impact, James gripped the steering wheel and jerked it to one side hoping to avoid the collision, and felt his stomach churn at the idea of him crushing her body beneath the wheels of his vehicle as the car came to a shuddering halt.

It took James a few moments to regain his composure and force himself to get out of the car to find out what had happened to her, at the same time wondering why the most beautiful woman he had ever set eyes on was standing in the centre of the long twisting road. In the wide open space of the snow covered North Yorkshire Moors.

'Oh God,' he muttered to himself, 'how could I have got myself into such a mess?'

With that thought in mind, James decided that he should go check on her and started to open the car door but lost his nerve. Instead, he chose to wind down the window and take a look from there.

To his surprise, as soon as he had lowered the window, he found himself gazing directly at her as she was standing beside the car. And to his relief she appeared to be uninjured.

For a few short seconds of him seeing her James felt all of the horrific past experiences slipping away. As their eyes met he was held mesmerised by her hypnotic, almond-shaped aquamarine eyes. James watched as her long flaxen hair mixed with the flakes of falling snow that swirled around her head, and the delicate, soft gossamer almost transparent, silk dress was whipped around her slender, perfectly shaped body.

Without a word she reached inside the car and touched the wetness on his forehead Then after giving a soft tinkling laugh she disappeared into the thick blanket of snow.

James sat motionless in the car stunned by the unexpected circumstances that had unexpectedly arisen. The last thing that he could recall was feeling the car skidding out of control on the slush covered road and coming to a halt on its side in a field. Then when he had clambered from the wreckage and looked inside the vehicle, he had stared in horror, as he saw his own blood soaked corpse. A grotesque look of disbelief was on its shattered face, his body impaled on the steering column.

In his panic to escape from the cottage, James had not secured his seat belt, with the force of the impact from the crash, his head had shattered the windscreen and he had bounced back onto the seat. The weight of his own body had then thrown him forward again and had impaled him onto the steering column, that had penetrated his chest and had gone directly into his heart.

For some peculiar reason the air bags had not inflated.

Chapter 53

GET HELP

The panic that had ensued after David's futile attempt to calm James, had failed and he had run from the chamber, David had turned to Tim, pleading with him to go get help.

Tim had hesitated because all that was fixed in his frustrated mind was the unnatural, hideous sight of the two motionless corpses of Bishop Johnson and Brother Armstrong kneeling in front of the statue. They were knelt as if paying homage to the long deceased Knight Templar.

He knew that whatever had taken their lives was still in in the confines of the macabre chamber. He was also concerned for David's safety and anxious about leaving him alone in the crypt.

Tim, who wasn't thinking clearly, was about to run upstairs and use the phone in the lounge to call the police, when he suddenly realised that he had his cell phone in his pocket and ground to a halt in the doorway of the passage.

"I don't have to go upstairs I can use my mobile!" he yelled, much louder than he anticipated, sending his voice echoing eerily about the shadowy recesses of the arches grotesque chamber.

Tim hesitated, and looking around at the weird carvings and paintings in the crypt he began to feel a sense of unease.

'Hell,' he cursed inwardly, as he felt his stomach starting to churn. He knew that something invisible was in there with them. But where? And what the hell was it?

"God, my nerves are shit," he cursed.

Tim felt his hands tremble as he fumbled for the phone in his pocket and didn't dare look at David as he dialled the local police station.

"Come on, come on," he mumbled, before finally being put through to the Chief Inspector to explain what had happened, and that there were two dead clergymen in the crypt.

For a few moments everything became silent until Tim shouted "What? What? are refusing to come, you bastard?" Then the line went dead.

Appalled, David stared in disbelief, when Tim flung the phone at the sarcophagus and watched as it smashed into pieces. Then, as if unable to cope with any more Tim dropped to his knees onto the cold stone flags rubbing his head, screaming and weeping with frustration.

Initially David was too shocked to do or say anything, then hurried to Tim's side and helped his distressed friend to his feet, asking what was wrong.

"I don't believe it," Tim shouted angrily. "The fucking Inspector said the cottage is cursed, and that he and his men can't take any chances, not after the fatalities that occurred the last time they came out here. They all blamed the deaths of their colleagues on their investigations here at the cottage. He's refused to come and help, and he's hung up on me," Tim moaned, shaking his head helplessly.

"Tim, listen to me," David said as he placed a sympathetic hand on his shoulder.

"Leave it with me."

"What can you do that I can't?" Tim snapped irritably.

"I can contact Bishop Edgar he will know what to do. In the meantime I suggest we get out of here and wait in the lounge. Then after I have spoken to the Bishop I am certain that he will sends us some help."

Reluctantly, Tim agreed, and gave a shudder after a final quick glance at the two corpses knelt in front of the giant statue. He followed David away from the chamber and locked the door securely behind them, turned off the light and they made their way back to the lounge.

David rang Bishop Edgar, to let him know that Bishop Johnson and Brother Armstrong were dead and tried to relate the dire circumstances of their deaths. He went on to tell him about the Ritual objects that they had found hidden inside the secret compartment at the base of the statue in the crypt. He also informed him that the two clergymen were facing the knight when found dead, and that there was an inverted cross of Christ.

At once Bishop Edgar was filled with alarm at their findings. He understood the true meaning of the items and wisely told David that on no account must he and Tim go near the chamber. He informed him that he would be contacting certain members of the Senate for assistance in the investigation and to wait for him to contact them.

Chapter 54

TENSION

It had taken Archbishop John Edgar two days to arrange for a special delegation of officials from the church to prepare for the removal of the two clergymen's bodies from the crypt.

Tim was exhausted, and while waiting for the Archbishop to make his decision, he had been drinking whisky non-stop and had now dropped off into a deep, restless sleep on the sofa. David sat waiting patiently, watching over him, waiting the Archbishop's secretary to contact him.

As twilight evening fell and night steadily approached, a peaceful serenity had fallen over David and he could feel his body starting to relax and his eyelids beginning to close.

He was almost asleep when he was unexpectedly pulled from his lethargic state by hearing strange guttural sounds coming from the hallway outside the closed door.

"Oh God," he whispered in a low tone as he crossed himself, "what now?"

David didn't want to disturb Tim, knowing that Tim's nerves were already stretched to the limit and he was almost at breaking point.

David realised he had to do something and fast, as he saw the door handle slowly turning. His automatic responses took over when in a flash, he pulled himself up from the chair, raced over to the door, turned the key and locked it.

Then staggered back when hearing an ungodly roar that emanated from something in the hallway, and watched in alarm as the door began to creak and groan vibrating beneath the tremendous pressure being forced down upon it.

"Oh shit," he murmured. For a moment David was too scared to move and stared helplessly at the door, then turned towards Tim, expecting him to have been awoken by the unexpected din. But Tim lay undisturbed by whatever was outside the lounge thudding and roaring like a mad animal.

"Loving Father protect and help me," he whispered as he fell to his knees and began praying deeply in earnest.

To David's relief, as he prayed, the din began to subside before falling into a bizarre silence that set his nerves on edge, and he stood waiting for the unexpected to occur.

But when it didn't, although he was quaking with diabolical fear, David felt himself fighting the urge to go and find out what was behind the door. But he couldn't, he was too afraid to move and he stayed where he was until he felt certain that nothing was waiting to pounce on him.

With his heart beating wildly, he turned the key and held his shoulder to the door ready to slam it shut if anything was waiting to grab him, and carefully inched it slightly ajar, giving himself just enough space to see if there was anything lingering in the hall, waiting for him to make the wrong move.

He was relieved to find that it was empty.

Chapter 55

WHAT IS IN THERE

David closed the door, locked it again and turned to Tim, who despite the upheaval had remained sound asleep. Not wanting to disturb him David found himself shaking so badly that he needed a drink, which was against his beliefs. He reached for the bottle of malt and poured himself a large drink, then hastily guzzled it down.

But he was still unable to relax and began pacing about the lounge. His main thoughts were centred upon the two clergymen and he began to wonder if they really were dead, or, could they have been in some kind of hypnotic trance?

If so, then they would be in desperate need of help.

No one had examined their bodies to check if they were dead or alive it had been assumed they were dead. But what if something really bad had scared them and they were in some form of hysterical paralysis?

With these tormenting thoughts flooding through David's mind, he decided that he would brave the elements and return to the crypt to find out if his two associates were still breathing. If so, then one way or another he would get them out of there.

But if not and the secret compartment had remained open, he would remove every one of the items inside and destroy them. Firstly he would try to find the reason for them being there and for what purpose were they being used.

Before he left David once again cast a worried eye over at Tim who lay snoring on the sofa, and decided not to disturb him. Whatever was down there, he would face it alone before placing anyone else in danger.

David opened the door and peered both left and right before moving out into the Hall. He cautiously edged his way along the corridor, with his back against the wall to protect himself from anything that could attack him from behind until he reached the basement door. Then with a shaking hand, he reached out, opened it and switched on the light.

Taking great care not to make any unexpected sound, he carefully made his way down the steps, crossed the games room and gym, then went through to the first crypt to where the low wooden door led down the steps and into the short passage to the second crypt.

David stopped for a few moments to gather himself together and took a deep breath before pressing the switch of the arc light and pushed open the door to enter the abysmal crypt.

"Father God bless and protect me," he murmured softly as he moved steadily forward, at the same time feeling his stomach churn at the sight of the two lone figures kneeling in front of the menacing statue in the dark shadows of the bizarre chamber.

Gathering all of the faith and strength he could muster, David uttered a silent prayer as he forced himself towards the motionless figures of the Bishop and Armstrong, then with a shaking hand he reached forward to check for a pulse in the Bishop's neck.

"Oh my God," he gave a gasp of alarm and quickly drew his hand away in shock when finding a slow, faltering pulse. The Bishop was still alive, but he appeared to be dead, as his body was rigid and cold as if in rigor-mortis. So how could this be? David felt a surge of fear race through him.

'I've got to get help,' he murmured, while at the same time removing his cell phone from his pocket. He began dialling 999 as he moved towards the door.

To his horror as he was about to go through, the door suddenly slammed shut and the light went out leaving him in utter and complete darkness.

"Oh no," he screamed. The emergency call was forgotten as he fumbled on his phone, to flick on the light, then shone the small beam directly about the confined and claustrophobic,space.

To his horror, he saw Bishop Johnson and Brother Armstrong slowly rise to their feet and with outstretched arms, they staggered towards him with demonic, menacing expressions on their faces.

Chapter 56

DAVID

Tim rubbed his eyes as he slowly edged himself upright on the sofa and sat groaning.

When he had awoken, the darkness in the room had surprised him as it had been early morning when he and David had entered the crypt and now it was almost midnight.

The last thing he could recollect was drinking whiskey when they returned to the lounge while David drank coffee as he tried to stay alert to what was happening.

As Tim struggled to bring back the past events, he remembered that at about 9-30am that morning he and David had been sifting through the old documents and photos that Jessica Howard had brought, and had allowed Julia to copy. They were now scattered about the table.

David had found something of importance when sifting through the old prints. He had noticed what appeared to be the ruins of a large house that was partially concealed by the trees in the forest and he had pointed it out to Tim.

The ruins of the mansion were hard to discern as whatever was left of it was scattered over the ground and almost covered by overgrown foliage and weeds. But after studying the picture for a while, David recalled hearing something of a large house having once stood in the centre of the forest.

He suddenly recalled that it was Bedlington Hall, near Leverton. He had seen it depicted in a number of historic paintings in the Harrogate arts section. He also discovered that after its last owners had met an untimely gruesome death, the Hall had succumbed to a blaze and had been destroyed by a vicious inferno that was believed to have been an arson attack that had razed the hall to the ground.

Beside the painting of the old hall was a portrait of the last owner, Lord Gerard Edgar Bartholomew, and beneath the portrait was a written documentation of the man who had originally resided at the Hall.

Lord Bartholomew had been a Knight Templar. He had been away from the country taking part in many skirmishes abroad. But after receiving serious injuries in the latest battle he had returned home to England and had settled down to live out his remaining years in the peace and tranquillity of country life.

There was no portrait of Lord Bartholomew with his wife, nor were there any single portraits of her. Strangely, there was no mention of Lady Bartholomew in the library, it was if she had never existed. Lord Bartholomew had died leaving no heir to the property and he was interred in the family tomb alongside his ancestors but not his wife.

It was presumed that Lady Bartholomew had returned to France her native country as nothing more was heard or written about her.

The information printed there stated that it was rumoured that Lord Bartholomew had been tutored in the black arts by spiritual leaders in foreign countries while he was living abroad.

'If that is correct; David had thought, then that would account for the occult paraphernalia that they had discovered in the cavity hidden behind the shield.

'This is getting very interesting,' he'd mumbled to himself he recalled that in the years following the fire, what was left of the hall had fallen into ruin and was reputed to be haunted by ghostly figures that had been seen floating about the derelict ruins.

171

It was also said that anyone who entered the forest would be corrupted by the evil influences remaining there. Therefore, everyone in the village avoided the forest and the surrounding land.

Nevertheless, part of the forest and land had been cleared a number of years later by the parish council who decided to build a church there.

"Shit," Tim mumbled, when suddenly understanding what David had been saying He wished that he hadn't drunk so much whisky on an empty stomach. His weak excuse had been that he was scared and needed a drink to calm his nerves. While David had used his senses, he had drunk coffee and eaten a hastily prepared sandwich.

But now it was too late, his conduct in a crisis was inexcusable Tim now found himself alone and in the dark, while the only light filtering through into the lounge came from the rays of the moon that were reflecting brightly across the glittering blanket of snow covered ground, and were sending glimmering shafts of light through the square panes of glass of the cottage windows.

Although Tim was still feeling the effects from the drink, he forced himself up from the sofa and felt his stomach churn as he made his way over to the window and looked outside.

Chapter 57

SHOCK

"Oh no," Tim groaned, when the sudden brightness from the moonglow on the stark white snow caught him unaware, forcing him to turn and race into the bathroom where he was violently ill.

"At least it's stopped snowing," he muttered to himself as he leant over the pan to throw up a second time. He moved over to the sink to splash cold water over his face to allow him to think more lucidly and he rinsed his mouth at the same time, ridding himself of the stale bitter taste lingering on his tongue. He was still feeling groggy when he returned to the lounge and plonked himself back down on the sofa and looked around hoping to see David.

But he was nowhere in sight.

'Where is the silly bugger? I hope he didn't go back down there on his own?' Tim grumbled as he leant over and switched on the table lamp that emitted a calming glow.

He glanced about the room once again, but there was still no sign of David.

'I thought he would have woken me up before now', Tim mumbled to himself, 'I hope to high heaven 'oh no,' he uttered when a terrifying thought crossed his mind.

'If he is down below on his own then I'd better get down there and help him.

But first I'll check to make certain that he isn't up here somewhere.'

Tim moved from one room to another calling David's name, but when there was no reply he went to the basement and called from the open doorway, but still there was no response.

"Shit, what the hell's he playing at?"

Reluctantly, Tim descended the stairs into the games room, then the gym and through the first crypt where he stopped and stared at the open door.

"I closed and locked that," he snarled, gritting his teeth until his jaw ached. "The stupid bastard must have taken the keys from my pocket while I was sleeping. "You bloody idiot." he cursed aloud.

Tim stood for a few moments, unsure of what to do then forced himself to proceed feeling his skin crawl at the thought of what he had seen the last time he'd entered the freaky, outlandish chamber. Cautiously, he made his way through the second doorway and down the stairs towards the second gruesome crypt.

As he did so, Tim immediately realized that there was no strong light emanating from within. Puzzled, he stood for a moment wondering what was wrong, he knew that the power was on as the switch was down so why was there no light coming from the crypt?

"Something's wrong here," he murmured under his breath as he noticed that only slight flickering spasms of light were emanating from the chamber, and cautiously peeped around the door.

For a few moments Tim couldn't believe his eyes as there were a number of candles set about the crypt that were creating weird dancing shadows on the walls.

What shocked him most was the sight of David cross legged and naked in the centre of a pentagram drawn in a circle of salt sitting with unrecognisable symbols completely covering his entire body.

Tim's mind whirled in confusion, before he managed to regain his composure and withdrew behind the door. He took in a number of deep breaths as he attempted to gather his wits and prepared a plan of action, knowing that he had to get David out of there and fast.

He realised that it was not going to be an easy task, when he forced himself to re-enter the crypt.

In the flickering darkness he saw that five black candles were burning at each point of the pentagram, and to his disgust each point had the inverted figure of Christ on the cross set in a pile of human faeces.

In front of David, set in the centre of the circle, was a small alter with wine and wafers as if ready for a communion service. However,what was making the scene even more obnoxious was a number of human bones and skulls set in its centre.

A silken tapestry had been draped over the sarcophagus where six black candles were burning in two silver candelabra that were placed at the head and feet of the sarcophagus. Between the two candelabra was a golden incense burner sending out billows of sickly unpleasant scented smoke.

Hanging on the wall behind the sarcophagus was the reverted cross of Christ, and suspended by a twisted red satin cord beside the Templar was a six feet long velvet, silk embroidered tapestry depicting the evil god Baphomet whom the Templars worshipped.

The entire chamber reeked of incense, human waste and decaying corpses.

In the few minutes that it took for Tim to take stock of what was in the chamber he noticed that everything had been removed from the cavity behind the Templar shield.

The two clergymen were both kneeling in a different position to where they had previously been, and were now facing the Templar statue, while David was uttering incantations in Latin.

Filled with fear of the unknown Tim backed away and quietly closed the door then locked it. He raced through the short passage and paused for a moment to lock that door also. He hurried across the basement and up the steps only stopping to close the door and secure it behind him. He then grabbed his coat from the hall cupboard and his car keys and hurried into the garage.

Then with every door locked behind him, Tim drove away from the cottage and called the police.

This time they could not ignore his desperate call, and were forced to go the cottage.

Chapter 58

DISBELIEF

Tim could hardly contain himself as the police station came into view, and he slammed his foot down hard onto the brake feeling its wheels bump up onto the kerb outside the building.

By now however, Tim was past caring about anything. All he could see in his mind's eye was the distressing sight of David and the two clergymen whom he believed to have been dead, knelt in front of the Templar statue chanting in some foreign language that he couldn't understand.

Distraught and breathless, he staggered into the police station, where the duty officer took one at his dishevelled appearance and rushed round his desk to assist Tim to a seat. It was obvious to the officer that Tim was in shock when he felt the chilling tremors running though his body and noting that his eyes were glazed and his speech incoherent.

But when Officer Brent became conscious that something more serios was amiss he started speaking to him in a soothing tone and called for immediate assistance.

It was only by chance that a doctor, who had been called in to attend a prisoner, was there to offer his assistance in helping Tim to overcome the devastating trauma to which he had been subjected.

It was unmistakably clear that Tim was in a state of shock, but the doctor had to gain his permission to allow him to administer a light sedative, which Tim gratefully accepted.

When a duty policewoman brought him a mug of hot sweet tea Tim had swallowed it down along with the pills, within minutes he sat back when feeling the sedative starting to ease the grief and pain of his guilty conscience. However It couldn't take away the certain knowledge that he was responsible for everything that had happened at the cottage.

He would never be able to forgive himself for the suffering that had been caused as well as the loss of his wife and dear friends, James and David. It would be a pain-filled memory that he would be forced to endure for the rest of his life.

Tears coursed down Tim's cheeks as he sat in a dazed, confused state of mind, until he suddenly becoming aware that Chief inspector Hudson was watching him.

"Please, please," he begged, "you've got to help them." He suddenly leapt to his feet and grabbing hold of the Chief Inspectors jacket.

Taken by surprise, Hudson jumped in alarm and grabbed hold of Tim in an arm lock rendering him helpless and from which he couldn't escape.

"Please," he implored, "you have to help them, they are being held prisoners in the crypt."

The chief Inspector looked over at Officer Brent, who gave a confused shrug and shook his head, he had no idea what crypt Tim was referring to.

"Who needs help?" Hudson asked, edging Tim back to the chair, seated him and let go of his arm.

What crypt are you talking about?"

Tim stared around at the anxious faces watching him.

"David, the Bishop, Brother Armstrong they're all trapped in the crypt." He was becoming hysterical again, but by speaking calmly the Chief Inspector managed to get Tim to explain in detail everything that was occurring at the cottage.

"I think we should take a look out there," Hudson suggested, helping Tim to his feet.

"Barnes, have my car sent round, and two more while you're at it, I want four men in each car, it sounds like trouble to me."

While they waited for the extra officers to arrive Tim noticed some of the looks of apprehension that passed between everyone in the interview room.

"Right" the Chief said, pulling on his overcoat and cap, "we had better get moving."

To everyone's surprise Tim handed the Chief Inspector the keys for every door oh the cottage telling him that he would never enter or go anywhere near the cottage again.

This didn't sit very well with the Chief Inspector who insisted that Tim go along with them. "After all' he stated, it was his home."

But Tim was adamant that he positively refused to go anywhere near the accursed property.

Chapter 59

THE POLICE

Locals in the tiny village of Galphay were awoken from their slumber in the early hours of the morning, by the sounds of sirens and the flashing lights of the police ambulances and fire engines as they raced towards Church Cottage.

The problem was that when the services arrived, there was no power to provide any electricity in the cottage, and for some strange reason the emergency generator was not working either. Therefore, the who area was in darkness and it made it extremely difficult for anyone to see what they were doing and where they were walking.

The first to arrive was Chief Inspector Hudson who immediately began bellowing instructions to his men. The problem was that although most of the officers knew about the hauntings and the gruesome deaths of their colleagues, occurring only a matter of weeks ago, they were hesitant about entering the property.

But after a severe rousting from Chief Inspector Hudson, Sergeant Baines promptly took the keys from him and unlocked the front door and herded his men inside.

Using their flashlights and following the directions that Tim had given them, they cautiously made their way along the hall until they reached the basement door that Sergeant Baines unlocked and opened. He recoiled in shock and almost forgot what he was supposed to be doing, when a repugnant, sickening stench belched from the open doorway completely enveloping him and the six officers accompanying him.

"What the hell!" Baines shouted, waving his arms about in an effort to waft the stink away. But as he tried to see what was happening, he realised that he and the officers were rapidly becoming enveloped in a blinding, dark, thickening mass.

"Oh my God," were the last words he ever spoke, when feeling something twist in his belly and looked down, where he saw an ornate silver dagger protruding from his gut and fell to the ground writhing in agony.

"Sergeant Baines, Serge where are you?" Officer Gordon called when hearing the agonising screams, and began groping his way through the dense mist towards the tortured howls of pain. Then stopped as he heard the weird gurgling sounds emanating all around him and listened, fully expecting to see something nearby' but there was nothing.

Trembling with fear of the unknown, Officer Gordon warily stepped toward the area from where the groans emanated, but instead of the feeling the carpet beneath his feet, he unexpectedly felt himself sliding on a slippery substance. Then as he attempted to regain his balance, Officer Gordon tripped over something lying on the carpeted hallway and found himself falling face down onto the floor.

For a moment or two the officer couldn't move, but when he did he instantly recognised the strong metallic odour of blood and he found himself staring down into the mutilated face of his friend, Officer Gerry Aldridge.

Gerry's throat had been slashed along with the four other colleagues from his unit.
All five of them lay on the floor bleeding profusely from gaping wounds severing their larynxes from ear to ear and almost severing their heads.

"Oh God, no" he muttered, then began screaming. "What the devil's going on in there?" Hudson shouted? hearing the hysterical shrieks.

The officers who were outside also heard the frantic cries from Officer Gordon, and assuming that he and his colleagues were in serious trouble, had raced inside.

But when coming face to face with the thick stinking fog inside the hallway, they had turned, and hurried outside to the riot vans where the gas masks were stored, and put them on, on the pretext that it could be some form of chemical they were dealing with.

Then had returned to push their way through the open door and into the hallway.

But as soon as they had entered the cottage the mist unexpectedly disappeared, revealing the mutilated bodies of the six officers lying in the blood-soaked hallway with officer Gordon lying, unconscious, amidst the bloody carnage directly in front of them, minus his hands.

Chapter 60

THE AFTERMATH

Everyone was in shock as they stood watching the traumatised, unconscious Officer Gordon being taken away in the wailing ambulance.

The forensic teams were already on their way and no one was allowed inside the cottage. Chief Inspector Hudson was having problems with the remaining teams of officers. After visualising the carnage that had occurred there none were willing to venture into the cottage. Subsequently when contacting the clergy, they had refused to make a passing comment regarding Bishop Johnson, Brother Armstrong and Brother David Hartley and didn't offer their services.

The press were a different matter; TV cameras were everywhere. Microphones on extended arms were stretched towards the police in an attempt to capture any words of information. Crowds of gory sightseers were gathering in hordes, all except the locals of course who had deliberately stayed away from the commotion.

People who were claiming to be psychics, were trying to gain attention from the media and TV stations, claiming were already in touch with the presence' inside' the cottage. Those people were ushered away by the police for their own safety.

The police were at a loss about what to do. In the meantime, Chief Inspector Hudson had ordered a cordon to be set encircling the property and a twenty four hour watch to be carried out. He also gave strict instructions that no civilian or police officer should cross the barrier and his men must keep a safe distance away from the cottage. If any of the crowd or media should manage to evade them and enter the property, then on no account must they go in after them.

Chief Inspector Hudson sat facing his superiors when holding the discussion about what decision they should make regarding the removal of the three clergymen trapped in the tomb. The clergy had made it clear that they didn't want any involvement regarding the problem and had adamantly refused to have a meeting with the police. It was, in their opinion, the police who should take complete charge and bring Bishop Johnson, Brother Armitage and Brother Hartley, out of the tomb. They would then be taken to a place of safety and helped to recover from their extraordinary ordeal.

That was easier said than done.

Over the following days, the police were inundated with ideas of how to help rescue the three trapped men. Who? due to the lack of oxygen, food and water they were assumed to be dead.

By a stroke of luck, Dennis Jones, a builder from York, had responded to one of the flyers that Tim had posted previously along with many others.

Dennis had been told where Tim was now residing, and had turned up one evening at the White Owl Pub asking for him.

Upon his arrival he introduced himself and told Tim that he had a proposal to make and could they talk somewhere in private. As the pub was fairly busy Tim ordered a couple of beers then took Dennis up to his room so they could be away from prying eyes and ears to listen to what Dennis had to say.

Once they were alone and settled, Dennis brought out a copy of the old drawings of the cottage that Tim had had duplicated. These had been dispatched to construction companies all around North Yorkshire, but it appeared that no one was willing or brave enough to tackle the job. Especially after the macabre incidents had been made public by the TV and media.

Dennis however, was adamant that he could carry out the work, saying that he didn't believe anything the media said or published, they always exaggerated the truth and would do anything to promote the sale of newspapers and to get viewers.

Tim agreed, and then shocked Dennis by stating that a film company The Paranormal Universe, had approached him with regard to filming inside the cottage and both crypts and the haunted area of the woods that belonged to Tim. The producer had told Tim that it would make a spectacular documentary, and that the public were always interested in hauntings and the paranormal. Especially where macabre incidents had taken place.

They were also interested if it was where black magic and the clergy were involved, and had offered to pay him over a million pounds for the rights to film there.

Dennis was stunned.

"If you did agree, he said, you would still have to get rid the property and whatever is in there?"

"I know that," Tim replied, huffily, getting to his feet and reaching for the house phone.

"I feel like having another drink, do you want one?"

"Yes, and a large scotch to go with it," Dennis replied, going over to the window and glancing out at the darkening sky.

"Shit" he groaned seeing a light flurry of snowflakes beginning to fall.

"I thought the blasted weather was going to improve."

"So did I." Tim came to his side and watched as the flakes became thicker as they fell rapidly covering the few vehicles parked in the grounds below.

"What do say to us going down and having something to eat?" Tim suggested.

"Its good grub and freshly made."

"You're on mate." Dennis said giving Tim a hearty slap on the back.

"Let's go eat and talk some more."

Chapter 61

THE MEETING

Tim and Dennis listened as word quickly spread about the pub that it had started snowing heavily again, and watched as the locals quickly downed their drinks and left knowing what to expect on the vast open moors. They wanted to avoid getting stuck in the snow with their vehicles, and those who were walking didn't want to get soaked to the skin.

Within half an hour the pub was almost empty, and the table by the blazing ingle nook fireplace was now vacant for Tim and Dennis to sit and enjoy their meal in comfort and warmth.

Tim had felt a twinge of sadness when recalling, that the last time that he'd eaten there had been with James. He had died due to his experience in the cottage and Tim was now blaming himself for that.

As he sat dwelling on his sad memories, he felt Dennis nudge him asking if he was alright.

"I'm sorry I was just thinking about my late friend James. What were you saying?" he stammered.

Dennis gave him a confused glance but not before he had observed the look of sadness that had descended on Tim's face.

"I was saying that if you wanted you could have the best of both worlds. First, you could get paid and let them do the filming, then if you were willing I would reimburse you, if you would allow my company to demolish both storeys of the cottage above the chamber.

"But," Tim began.

"Please hear me out." Dennis then went on to explain.

When both storeys are down at ground level we would shift the rubble and use a JCB to dig a deep wide trench alongside the remaining wall at the back of the cottage.

This would be wide and deep enough to enable six men to shore up the remaining soil with sheets of ply and strong timbers to protect the team who would be working there next.

He explained that they would first chisel through an area and place a supporting beam in the stone wall of the chamber. Then, when the wall had been secured, they would next knock out a space in the stonework high and wide enough for the crew to get through and bring out the three corpses.

Then if everything went as planned they would fill in the chamber with rubble from the cottage.

The plan sounded plausible enough to Tim, but he had a lot to lose. Tim had spent almost every penny he owned in purchasing and renovating the cottage, and was concerned whether he could afford to allow the partial demolition to proceed.

He was reluctant to return there and felt that he had no option other than to do what Dennis was suggesting. Even if it did mean demolishing part of the cottage.

Whatever happened to the property Tim had made up his mind to forget about it even if it meant leaving it to fall into ruin.

'But what if that area was demolished and filled in?' he wondered. 'Would that get rid of the curse, and would I be able to return and live there in peace?'

Then a thought crossed his mind causing him to shudder. What about the ghosts in the woods it wouldn't get rid of those would it?' 'Oh bloody hell what am I going to do?' he thought rubbing his head in frustration.

To Tim's surprise and disbelief, he could hardly believe what he was hearing when Dennis offered him a substantial amount of money to purchase the whole area; cottage, woods and all, as well as reimburse him for all of the furnishings and whatever had been left behind.

Tim could hardly believe his luck with the substantial offer the film company had made, and as no one else had come forward with an offer to purchase the property, Tim realised that he could make a tidy sum. When the time came he would have enough finances to retire with ease.

He was however, being pressurised by the local authority to do something about the publicity of the deaths and the weird phenomena coverage that was occurring in that area of North Yorkshire. Also the problem of the rotting corpses of the three clergymen who still remained entombed in the second crypt, and were now a health hazard and should be removed immediately, according to the public health department.

Tim could hardly believe the council's complaints, after all, news of the haunting had brought in much needed revenue to the area. Along with it being publicized world-wide, sight, seers from all corners of the globe were arriving in droves wanting to see or stay in the haunted cottage in the hope of seeing the ghosts.

The clergy however were a different matter, they were insisting that Tim himself should arrange to bring out the priests remains as it was his property they were entombed in. But Tim's lawyer, Roger Dwyer, had informed the clergy that they should arrange for the removal of their own members of the church themselves.

But they clergy, had articulated, that Tim must arrange for the body's removal.

In other words they were too scared to enter the crypt and do it themselves.

Chapter 62

FAMILY PARTING

Because of all the problems that had arisen, Tim was eager to sell the whole area and property to the builder, Dennis Jones. He was only too pleased to be ridding himself of the accursed, property and to start a new life many miles away from there.

But before Denise Jones could start any work, there was the legal aspect to think of.

Tim contacted his lawyer Roger Dwyer to have an agreement drawn up and a bill of sale for the cottage, land, and part of the forest, where Jones was hoping to construct a small housing estate with shops and other amenities.

To Tim's dismay within a matter of days for the legal exchange of the property being signed over to Dennis Jones. Tim's lawyer had called informing him that there had been numerous incidents reported on the abandoned property.

Tim had felt the bile rise in his stomach at the merest mention of the cottage, and asked what the problems were.

Roger told him of the horrendous apparitions and weird phenomena, plus the ghost sightings that were rumoured to be regularly occurring both inside and outside of the cottage. Not only that, but there were a number of so called mediums and psychic investigators who were constantly trying to break into the deserted property who were being injured by an unseen force, some seriously.

Tim had grimaced when hearing what Roger was saying, because he believed that all of his problems would have been over after he had agreed to sell the property to Dennis Jones. Shouldn't the complaints have gone directly to him?

Roger then went on to explain that the cottage and surrounding lands were still his until the property had been signed over to the purchaser.

'Can it get any worse, Tim grumbled, throwing down the book he had been reading and began pacing the floor.

By allowing the movie company to film inside the cottage, the proceeds had allowed Tim to purchase and settled in a decent sized bungalow standing in its own grounds. It had acres of open moorland surrounding it near the Grimwith reservoir.

Not only was the distressing scenario growing worse, but his daughter, Annabella, had decided that after the horrendous death of her mother she was to accept her aunt Francesca's invitation and go live with her in Australia. She said that she would not be returning to England.

Rupert had gone to the USA to complete his training and had decided to stay there. In other words, Tim was left depressed and alone, with only photographs and his sad memories to remind him of the once happy family he'd had.

He knew that the children blamed him for their mother and James' death when they said that they didn't want any part of the past to remind them of how happy they had once been.

Tim had been left on his own to sort out any problems whatsoever that may have arisen and come his way.

Tim's thoughts were suddenly interrupted when only half an hour had passed before his lawyer rang again. This time it was Roger Informing him that Dennis Jones had called to say, that he had booked a suite and arranged for all three of them to meet at The White Owl pub within the next two days. And he should bring an overnight bag as they may be staying to work out a solution to the problems that had arisen.

Chapter 63

THE UNDEAD

Tim packed his camcorder, camera and recording device in the specially designed metal carry case he used for his work, along with a holdall containing extra clothing that he may be needing for the next few days. He then sat back waiting as the time ticked slowly by.

Thursday morning came, the snow was gone but it was cold and blustery with spasms of pouring rain.

Tim was filled with apprehension as he packed his gear into his four wheel drive BMW then set off on the B6 160 towards the small community near Appletreewick.

When he arrived at The White Owl Pub he was pleased to see Roger waiting for him in the lounge, he got to his feet and greeted Tim warmly. Thankfully, Roger had ordered the steak pie with veg and within minutes of his arrival Tim and Roger were tucking into plates filled with hot food and a number of drinks on the table. They did however, wait until they had finished eating before Tim told him of the conversation he'd had with Dennis Jones, the property developer from York, and the film company's proposition.

"If I were you," Roger said thoughtfully, "I would first allow the film company to carry out whatever filming they require. Then sell the entire property lock stock and barrel to the developer, that for some untold reason Mr Jones appears eager to own.

"It's strange you should say that," Tim added pensively. He had also begun having his doubts regarding the builder and was wondering what he was up to.

"Does he know something about the property that I don't? no it would have shown up on the documents that Jessica had brought." Tim shrugged off his suspicions.

Roger then told him that he had arranged for them to meet Dennis Jones at the site on Friday morning at 9am.

Tim could hardly believe his ears, both Roger and Dennis knew that he was reluctant to return to the property, and he told Roger that he would rather hold the discussions at the pub. But Roger was adamant that they held the discussion on site as there were certain problems that needed to be sorted out and wouldn't hear of it being held elsewhere. He also asserted that Tim must personally attend the meeting.

Friday morning heralded a bright calm day when Tim and Roger arrived early to meet the developer on site. To Tim's surprise it took only half an hour for Roger and Dennis to reach an agreement, and to be honest, Roger could hardly believe what he was hearing when Dennis agreed, without any objection, to the price that Tim was asking.

Dennis thought that it was a fair and reasonable price and suggested that he and Roger go into the cottage to sign the papers that Roger was carrying in his briefcase.

Roger however, was reluctant to enter the cottage and informed Dennis that he could sign the necessary documents either at the pub or in his car, the choice was his.

For some obscure motive Dennis chose the car.

Tim watched as the men got into the back of Roger's car and he observed Roger take a number of papers from his briefcase and hand them to Dennis.

Meanwhile, just out of boredom and to help pass the time, Tim decided to go for a walk to ease the tension that had built up inside him while the finalization of the sale was being completed. But for some unknown reason he had found himself wandering almost ankle deep through the fallen leaves of the forest well away from the area that he had previously owned.

As Tim brushed away the dead twigs and brambles that pulled at his clothing, he forced his way forward until he reached a beautiful, open glade where the rays of the sun had broken through the budding branches of the trees and were now shining down onto, a large brightly glowing patch of fresh crisp green grass.

For a few moments he stood gazing in awe at the incredible, unusual sight, thinking that the grass should have been dull and flat at this time of year. Then suddenly felt his body go incredibly tense when a strong shudder of untraceable fear raced through him.

"Oh my God, what's happening?" he screamed with fright feeling a sense of untold horror begin to surround him.

Glancing about he saw nothing untoward, but when he spun completely around he felt his flesh crawl, when he saw a group of approximately, twenty young girls aged between twelve to about fourteen year old that he assumed must have followed him there.

The next thing he became aware of was that the glowing copse had lost its lustrous colour, and was now becoming dim and dull as if night was closing in.

Unable to understand what was happening, Tim glanced towards the girls but when he looked at them closely, he was astounded to see that they were all heavily pregnant.

For a few moments Tim didn't dare move and he stared at the girls not knowing what to do, before following their gaze up to where they pointing. Then he drew in a sharp intake of breath as he saw two naked headless men's corpses, with their hands bound behind their backs, suspended by a rope tied around their feet hanging from the nearby trees.

At that moment Tim was paralyzed with fear unable to call out or move until he felt someone standing beside him calling his name.

"Tim? Tim old boy, are you alright?" he heard through a blistering haze of confusion.

"What," he managed to utter.

"I said are you alright, you look as if you have just seen a ghost?"

Tim look towards Roger who was staring at him with a look of concern on his face.

"You look like hell, come on Dennis wants to talk about the land."

"No," Tim stammered, "Did you see them? You must have seen them?" Tim was shaking from head to toe from the shocking sight he'd just seen.

"See who? What are you talking about?" Roger asked, taking Tim's arm and trying hard not to alarm him as he gently edged him towards the open ground.

"Those girls and the men up there." Tim could hear his voice rise in hysteria as he pointed toward the trees.

"There's no one up there, come on man get a grip on yourself," Roger said harshly.

Dennis wants to have a word with you, he wants your opinion in clearing part of the forest, he said that if he could get planning, he would put in an offer to buy it from the Church then clear most of it and build there."

Chapter 64

PLANNING

It took three months for the planning permission to go through allowing Dennis to build, and to purchase and clear the rest of the forest standing on the church land.

Meanwhile, after consulting their lawyers, Police Chief Inspector Hudson made a statement to the press and Demonic Productions, that on no account would any member of the police force be held accountable for whatever occurred when they were carrying out their assignments. And that for their own safety, none of his officers must enter the cottage.

The same applied to Dennis Jones' work crew, when carrying out the attempted rescue of the three trapped men. He alone would be held responsible for the safety of every man carrying out the dangerous task of removing the bodies from the crypt.

Following this statement, several days later a crew of workmen began the demolition process of the entire cottage. When this was completed another team was brought in with a JCB to dig a deep trench at the rear of the property.

There was however, a stumbling block, as the three dead people, one of who was a high ranking member of the clergy were trapped in the crypt. Also the crypt was still regarded as hallowed ground. This meant that Dennis would have to wait until he was given permission from the church to break into the crypt and bring out the putrefied remains of the three dead men.

But the question remained, who would be willing to go into the haunted crypt and remove the bodies that would be in a bad state of decay and stinking by now.

The only answer that Tim and Roger could think of would be to approach a group of disbelievers about the Christian religion. But the puzzling question was where would they find them?

Tim recalled that he had been appalled by what David had said about the Duke, Gerard Bartholomew. He had been a Knight Templar who had studied many different forms of religions and the workings of ritual magic in the Far East.

After being seriously wounded in one of the battles there, he had returned home to recuperate, and as he regained his strength Gerard had found the time to meditate on what he had learnt while abroad.

He had then blended all of the beliefs and myths and mystic sorcery together from each country to create his own religion and had acquired many faithful followers. The trouble was that his beliefs included everything that was perverse and degrading to the human race. He and his followers used helpless children, women and men against their wills for their diverse sexual satisfaction in situations that were against the true Christian belief.

"That's it!" he cried, when the idea suddenly came to him.

"Roger, I've got it, the only people who can remove the three bodies from the crypt without being harmed, have to be strong believers in the occult. They have to have the same beliefs as to those of the Duke."

Roger was astounded by what Tim was hinting at as the thought had never crossed his mind.

"Where the hell are we going to find anyone like that?"

"I don't know" Tim replied, giving a helpless gesture with his shoulders. "You should know better than me, what with you being a lawyer. You are always coming across all sorts of degenerates and perverted weirdos, aren't you?"

Roger's face was blank he was absolutely clueless and didn't know what to suggest.

"I'll tell you what, seeing as Jones appears to be eager to get in there," Tim added thoughtfully, "why don't we let him."

Chapter 65

CANABALISM

Dennis Jones could hardly believe his luck when he was given permission to enter the crypt. The first thing he did was to dig out at the rear of the cottage and make it safe for his six chosen men to break through the stone wall. This would enable them to enter the crypt and bring out the bodies.

The church senate insisted that as soon as they entered the crypt they must record and film every last detail of what was in the tomb before bringing out the bodies. Also, there must be no other copies made for the builder's personal use.

Dennis was only too pleased to oblige, he would be the first to enter the crypt when it was opened, but there would be more than one camera filming what was in there despite the clergy insisting that only one copy should be made.

Within an hour of a gap being made in the stone wall, exposing whatever was inside the crypt, the large arc light was pushed through the hole. It lit up the complete area inside and Dennis and Brian began filming. But when the cameras swept across to one corner of the crypt the lens revealed a sight that only the strongest of stomachs could endure.

"Bloody Hell," Dennis gasped, almost dropping the camcorder and turned his head away as the men clambered inside behind him with three plastic body bags.

"Get out quick!" he yelled.

But it was too late, the men had already caught a glimpse of the revolting sight and were rapidly scramble back the way they had come unable to believe what they were seeing.

But for Dennis, time momentarily seemed to be standing still as he stared in shock at the abhorrent sight of David's decaying corpse propped in a corner of the crypt.

His eyes had sunk into the skeletal bone structure of his face, and the skin covering the lower part of his jaw had rotted away exposing teeth and bones where his cheeks should have been.

Dried vomit and intestines covered the cold stone-flagged floor. Worse was to come when Dennis saw that David's naked body was layered with dried blood, from feeding from the corpses of Bishop Johnson and Brother Armstrong in an attempt to stay alive.

The two men lay naked with their genitals missing while the rest of their remains were showing a number of teeth marks in them. These had torn the skin after biting the flesh, leaving bones and broken, white ribs protruding from their bloody corpses.

"Fucking hell," he murmured, before emptying the entire contents of his stomach onto the ground where he was standing. He then slowly backed away until he was clear of the crypt and joined his men on level ground outside.

Chapter 66

VOLUNTEERS

"There was no way Dennis was going back into that hell hole and contacted Roger to tell him of his findings, and that if the synod didn't find someone to bring out the bodies within two weeks. He would be filling in the crypt and burying the bodies with the rubble that he would be shovelling in there.

Roger was stunned by the news and without hesitation he contacted the Archbishop, who informed him that an emergency meeting would be held immediately to arrange whatever was necessary to remove the three clergymen.

It didn't take long for someone to leak the news to the media about what had occurred at the cottage. But the reporters who had been amongst the throng when the phenomena first broke out there, were reluctant to enter the building to acquire font page news for their paper, neither were the television reporters.

The news had been seen on TV all over the country, and to the surprise of everyone watching, the first people to offer assistance came from Armley Jail, Leeds.

The offer came from a number of hardened criminals who expressed their willingness to help in the removal of the dead men on condition that the crown would considered them for an early release. They stated they had strong stomachs and weren't easily disturbed by the sight of a rotten corpse nor were they scared of ghosts.

'Easier said than done.' Dennis muttered to himself when Roger gave him the news.

It took a couple of frustrating days of waiting to arrange an emergency meeting between Dennis Jones, the clergy and prison officials before it was finally agreed to allow six of the most trusted prisoners to enter the crypt and bring out the corpses, and to have their sentences reduced.

They were forewarned about what could happen to them once they were inside the crypt and to be prepared for the nauseating sight of what they would be facing.

The leader would be handed a camcorder to film whatever was inside the chamber, including the three corpses.

'That's if they manage to stayed inside long enough to do any filming,' Dennis thought to himself, 'or survive.'

Regardless of what may occur in the crypt, there would be a number of armed guards in attendance to ensure the prisoners did not attempt to escape.

Chapter 67

QUESTIONS

Each of the prisoners, Peter Yang, Brian Harston, Mike Prentis, Jerry Maguire, Harry Abbot, and Leo Silver, were kitted out with cameras, that the C.I.D. investigating team had inserted into the headsets each prisoner would be wearing. This would be leaving them hands free in case of any problems that may arise, and to enable them to remove any obstacles that they could come across while in the crypt.

The cameras would also enable the police to monitor what was in the crypt, and hear what the men were describing as they went along. Then when all was made ready three of the six men were handed body bags and shovels in preparation for bringing out the corpses.

To the men's surprise they were each given a large dram of whiskey. This, they were told was to give them extra courage in facing whatever was down there.

The men gave one another a look of concern due to the unexpected offering, and began whispering to one another. They were now uncertain about the task they were to undertake.

Harry Abbott began questioning the Prison Governor, Brad Peters, about the possible danger that could be awaiting them.

But he was told not to be alarmed everything regarding their security had been taken care of, and there was no reason for any of them to be concerned.

Nevertheless, four of the six men had now become uneasy and were having second thoughts about entering the chamber. They felt that they hadn't been given enough information about what to expect once they were inside and much to the annoyance of the higher command, they held back from taking a step further.

'For goodness, sake,' Brad Peters cursed under his breath, as he felt an unexpected surge of anger flare up at the men, 'what the hell was wrong with them?'

They had agreed to bring out the bodies for a lesser sentence, and not only that but he'd had to approach the chief magistrate to explain and convince him of the horrific situation they were in, and that the only offers of assistance had come from the six prisoners in exchange for an early release. But now they were hesitating and asking questions about why the church, the police, and the funeral directors were unwilling to enter the chamber and bring out the bodies.

What was in there that they were all afraid of?

Chapter 68

NO ESCAPE

It had taken hours of patient discussions between all groups to convince the prisoners that every precaution had been taken to ensure their safety.

Two of the men, Brian Harston and Jerry Maguire, had refused to carry out the task and had been escorted back to Armley Jail. The other four had only one thought in mind, and that was to achieve a reduced sentence and earn an early release from prison.

They had reluctantly prepared themselves for the daunting assignment they were about to undertake.

By the time they were ready to go below ground, a large group of sightseers, newspaper reporters and television crews were surrounding the property perimeter, waiting in eager anticipation at the hope of seeing something phenomenal occur.

The Chief Inspector gave Harry Abbot, the leader of the prisoners, a final rundown of what he and the men were expected to do. The top priority being was to film everything in the crypt then bring out the three bodies. Afterwards, they would be returned to the prison until the prison Board of Directors had decided on the reduction of their sentences. When all of this had been explained to them and he was assured that they fully understood, Dennis Jones led them down the slope at the rear of the demolished cottage to the opening leading into the crypt.

He wished them good luck and made a hasty departure back to the safety of higher ground. From where he started the generator and switched on the portable arc light that he and his men had left behind in their mad dash to escape after seeing what was inside the crypt.

The four men looked down at their feet as they kicked away pieces of the remaining rubble before entering through the breach in the wall. As soon as they entered the crypt and they took in their surroundings.

They were totally unprepared for the appalling and horrendous sight of David's partially decomposed, naked, blood-smeared corpse. The half-eaten skeletal remains of the two clergymen who lay in the centre of a blood stained pentagram, along with fragments of gnawed human bones that were strewn about the floor.

"Fucking hell," Harry cursed, before emptying the entire contents of his stomach onto the dried blood spotted ground, and had to lean against the wall for support when feeling his knees turning to jelly. Leo had taken one look and dropped to the floor in a dead faint, while Peter and Mike had beaten an astonishingly fast retreat and were outside with the police in seconds, gabbling incoherently about what they had seen below.

Harry the toughest man of the group was trying to keep his wits about him, and had leant over Leo, slapping his face in an attempt to bring him round.

Within minutes though, as Leo began regaining his senses he became hysterical, and as Harry tried to calm him by using his body as a shield to stop him from seeing the carnage scattered about them. Leo began struggling to free himself from Harry's strong grip yelling that they had to get out of there.

Above ground, the officials were appalled by what was being recorded on the TV screens. They watched as Harry slowly moved about the chamber filming the macabre sight of the corpses and casting weird shadows when passing across the beam of the arc light as he stumbled over the scattered fragments of candles, crosses, chalice and the upturned self-made altar. Leo reluctantly filmed the paintings of the unrecognisable saints, the sarcophagus, the embroidered tapestry of Baphomet and the inverted cross of Christ.

Harry Abbott, felt the tears sting his eyes when seeing the cross. For a few moments, he recalled that he'd had a strong Christian upbringing. But in his late twenties he had left the church behind and taken to drinking and a life of crime which he had later regretted; when discovering that money and brute force wasn't everything that his new group of acquaintances had made it out to be.

At the moment Harry decided that he was going to turn his life around, he was going back to the church and make his mother proud of him, instead of hanging her head in shame whenever his name was mentioned.

His reverie was abruptly broken when a loud voice crackled in his ear, telling him to get on with the job he was supposed to be doing.

Harry could feel his anger rise, 'what the hell' he seethed, 'they weren't down here in this godforsaken stinking place where he was. They were in the sanctity of open ground above.

Harry forced himself to calm down knowing that it was losing his temper that had pushed him over the edge in the first place and had got him into prison. As a youth the goading from gangs had been about him being too soft, and had led to him into trouble which there was no escape from.

Once again the harsh sound of Hudson's voice rang in his ears telling him to get on with it, leaving Harry no option but to begrudgingly begin filming the opening behind the Templar shield.

Leo, who had been aiming his camera towards a dark recess near the sarcophagus, called to Harry, when he thought he had seen a figure pass the through the far wall.

At first Harry though it was Leo's imagination until he heard Hudson's voice in his ear saying that he had seen the figure and was asking who it was.

Harry had no idea and swung his head from left to right hoping to see the elusive figure but there was nothing. Hudson who was watching it on the screen above whispered a warning to Harry that it was almost behind him.

Harry spun round shining his torch directly in front of him, but he still couldn't see anything. Unexpectedly, he felt himself being held in a firm iron grip that tightly squeezed as it grasped him around the throat and lifted him into the air.

Within seconds Harry could feel himself choking but before he took his final breath he was released and came crashing down to the ground with such an almighty thud that it forced the wind from his lungs.

His ordeal wasn't over. As he lay on the ground, terrified and thoroughly winded, he watched in horror as the marble lid of the sarcophagus slid to one side then fell onto the hard flagged ground and shattered into pieces.

"Oh my God," Harry whispered, feeling his throat constrict with fear. At that moment he expected something to climb out of the sarcophagus and grab him. Thankfully nothing did.

For a few moments Harry didn't dare move and he lay trembling and shaking in absolute dread at what would happen next. He rose unsteadily to his feet and shone his torch light about the dark recesses of the chamber searching for Leo. But there was no sign of him.

"The fucking coward" he snarled. Then did a double take when he heard Hudson telling him to leave the bodies and get out of there, fast. But before Harry could make a move he felt an invisible force dragging him down onto the floor, and a great weight being pushed against his now helpless form. He saw the glint of the approaching knife only seconds before it entered his chest.

Everyone watching the monitors above ground screamed as they witnessed the appalling sight of David's festering, decayed, cadaver rise to its feet and stagger with outstretched arms across the bloody floor to where Harry lay.

They saw the dark outline of a man reach into the open wound of Harry's chest and pull out Harry's still pulsating heart and placing it into David's outstretched claw-like hands. Who pushed it into his bony jaws and with great relish devoured it.

"Oh my God!" someone screamed loudly amongst the mayhem and confusion.

"Where's Leo Silver?"

"He must have escaped," another called.

"No, look at the monitor," Hudson's voice quivered as he spoke.

All eyes turned towards the screen. "Oh my God, Peter Yang moaned leaning against Hudson for support.

On the monitor and in full view for everyone to see, were the remains of Leo who had been hacked to pieces and was laid in a massive swirling eddy of blood. The two decayed corpses of Bishop Johnson and Brother Armstrong who were covered with Leo's warm blood, were knelt alongside him, eagerly devouring chunks of flesh from his slashed and lacerated body.

Chapter 69

THE MYSTERY CAMERAMAN

The relatives of the deceased men were totally unconcerned regarding the news of their son's and brothers, deaths, and didn't care what happened to them.

Leo Silver, and Harry Abbot were well known to the police, and had always been a problem since childhood. They had spent most of their lives in and out of institutions until ending up in prison together for the murder of an elderly couple in Normanton, West Yorkshire.

Brian Harston and Jerry Maguire were taken back to Armley Jail, along with Peter Yang and Mike Prentis, who believed they'd had a lucky escape.

The Bishop, Brother Armstrong, and the Reverend David Hartley, were a different matter, their close relations and the church officials agreed that a quiet ceremony be held in respect for all the good work they had done in the past.

However, when Chief Inspector Hudson had gathered everyone concerned to see the recordings of the investigation of the crypt being replayed, they were shocked and alarmed to see that after Abbott and Silver had met their demise, someone had videoed inside the sarcophagus. Its heavy, marble effigy of the woman had been smashed and strewn about the floor.

This deliberate act of destruction had revealed a coffin of solid mahogany with its lid gaping wide open. The contorted remains of a woman lay in a gown of cream silk and lace, who, from all appearances, had been buried alive.

The blood stains on the torn satin material lining the coffin and her broken finger nails suggested that she had tried desperately to claw her way out.

Hudson frowned and was baffled, knowing there had been no one left alive to film the gruesome yet sad discovery. The only way that he could think of that someone could have filmed the sarcophagus and the cruel sadistic deaths of Abbott and Silver, was that Prentis must have lost his head gear when he ran screaming from the crypt in panic.

But the enigma was, who had picked up the camera and continued filming? It certainly wasn't Harry Abbott, nor Leo Silver, they were both dead.

Chapter 70

THE FINAL OUTCOME

In only a matter of hours a decision was made amongst the hierarchy that whatever was in the chamber was a danger to mankind. Police, Clergy and civilians had died in the cottage grounds, whereby it was decided that what was left of the building should be filled and sealed as soon as possible along with the remains of the dead.

Due to the hyped that the media had created, the local MP, Eric Watson, had become involved regarding the supernatural and macabre happenings.

The MP had then taken advice from higher authorities, and it was agreed that it would be best to get rid of the problem by detonating the building and destroying it before there was a further loss of lives.

The builder, Dennis Jones, was allowed to arrange for a demolition company to be brought in and send a robotic device into the deadly crypt with enough explosives to bring down the roof to seal and bury the invisible, deadly force inside the chamber.

The day of the demolition was a find Tuesday morning but overcast, and the whole area had become a mass of howling TV and newspaper media, vying against one another to be the first to film the destruction of the cottage.

When the red flag went up, the warning wail of the siren was the only sound heard, everyone fell silent knowing that the destruction of the crypt and everything inside was about to take place. When it did, a loud burst of cheers erupted from the watching crowd of bystanders that could be heard above the din of falling masonry, as the remnants of the remaining building collapsed into the ground.

For a while all was quiet as everyone peered anxiously into the clouds of swirling dust. They watched and waited for the unexpected to happen as it settled slowly on top of the debris. Suddenly the air was filled with the sound of roaring engines as both police and media helicopters flew overhead, but the onlookers were more interested in what was happening in front of them. They turned their attention to the tipper lorries, loaded with rubble who were starting to fill in the remaining uneven ground. Then massive bulldozers began levelling the complete area.

After the whole area was completely covered with rubble and levelled, Dennis Jones began making his preparations for completing his new village. Leaving everyone believing that this would be the end to all their problems.

No one had seen the malevolent force that had been released by the explosion.

THE END BUT NOT THE END

Acknowledgements

Firstly, I would like to show my appreciation to Michele, my proof reader, who has improved my use of grammar and pronunciation.

Secondly, I wish to thank my husband Eric who has had to suffer reading my horror stories. He did, however, help me tremendously with our family history of true war stories.

He never complained about the danger that I was putting myself in when I went out to investigate haunted sites at night with our daughter, Lesley Anne.

Thirdly I am grateful to Lesley Anne for her assistance in staying by my side no matter how nerve racking the situation became.

Books also written by the Author

FICTION

DARK OAKS

GATEWAY TO HELL

THE LAKE

FACT

BEFORE AND THROUGHOUT WW 1 & WW 2
TO THE PEACETIME OF THE PRESENT DAY

TRUE STORIES OF THE PARANORMAL

RESTLESS SPIRITS

SEEING IS BELIEVING

Back page of the Book

When Julia, Tim's wife dies of fright after seeing weird ghoulish apparitions in their new home, Church Cottage, Tim asks for help from the local police.

When there are multiple unexplained deaths and all efforts to obtain help are refused, Tim calls on his friend David Hartley, the vicar from the parish where he used to live.

When things go wrong two higher ranking church members are sent to investigate the mysterious happenings at Church Cottage. They are unexpectedly attacked by an invisible being and left for dead in the depths of the newly discovered sinister crypt.

Seeing the news on TV, six prisoners of Armley Jail, Leeds offer to go into the crypt and bring out the three bodies in return for a reduction in their prison sentences.

Their offer is accepted, but when they enter the crypt they discover traces of cannibalistic ritual black magic, then there are more dead bodies!

Photo of the author

Ingram Content Group UK Ltd.
Milton Keynes UK
UKHW012211080523
421345UK00003B/71

9 781803 696546